Night in Tunisia

NEIL JORDAN

NIGHT IN TUNISIA

BRANDON

MP1779 — Night in Tunisia cp

This edition 1982
Brandon Book Publishers Ltd
Dingle, Co. Kerry, Ireland

First published in 1976
by the Irish Writers' Co-operative

© Neil Jordan 1976, 1982

ISBN 0 86322 002 9

Cover design: Brendan Foreman

Printed in Great Britain by
Photobooks, Bristol

INTRODUCTION

by Sean O'Faolain

This is a highly original, personal, distinctive and interesting book. What more can one ask of any book except that it should be written by a man who also has the gift of words, images, feelings, responsiveness? Neil Jordan shows all these qualities. If he keeps and develops his primal gifts — he is quite young; barely 25 when this first collection of stories appeared — he will become an outstanding writer. At present he is intensely concerned with things of the mind and spirit rather than with the social world in which most of us spend most of our busy lives, but he is also tremendously responsive to all the things, people, surroundings and influences that have affected him as a youth — which is precisely how one would also describe the relationship of Joyce to his world in *Portrait of the Artist as a Young Man*. A further cause for special interest in Neil Jordan is that while being thus engrossed in his locale he is in no way, as Joyce also was not, in the least bit parochial or regionalist. In fact, surprisingly and delightfully, the hero of the central story of this group of stories is

American jazz music, the objective correlative of his theme is an alto saxophone and its presiding deity is old Charlie (Bird) Parker. In harmony with the mood of this music Jordan concentrates on the sexual growth of a very real boy through his relationship with a very real girl, who like himself is a life-yearner, as well as one the watchful father, one of the last of the old brass-men. In the course of that tale music releases the youth to life, to love, to selfhood. This kind of metaphor and symbol is a new and releasing thing in Irish literature. It is a personal language. It has no echo of the worn out, now rather boring old language and symbolism of rural Ireland's little white-washed country cottages, her wet winding roads, her colleens driving home the cows, her old priests, the little country chapel, the patriotic songs and laments of country pubs. This young man's metaphors are songs like *The Crying Game, The Tennessee Waltz, Night in Tunisia,* a boy fingering an old piano in a dance hall, the sax wailing high, and out there beyond the tin hut where he and his father live, enclosed and alone, the dusk, the waves on the beach, the night, the girl, the world, the future.

CONTENTS

ACKNOWLEDGEMENTS

New Irish Writing, Stand, London Magazine, Best Irish
Stories, ed. David Marcus, (Paul Elek), Icarus, Journal
of Irish Literature, St Stephens.

To Vivienne Shields

LAST RITES

One white-hot Friday in June at some minutes after five o'clock a young builder's labourer crossed an iron railway overpass, just off the Harrow Road. The day was faded now and the sky was a curtain of haze, but the city still lay hard-edged and agonisingly bright in the day's undiminished heat. The labourer as he crossed the overpass took note of its regulation shade of green. He saw an old, old negro immigrant standing motionless in the shade of a red-bricked wall. Opposite the wall, in line with the overpass, he saw the Victorian facade of Kensal Rise Baths. Perhaps because of the heat, or because of a combination of the heat and his temperament, these impressions came to him with an unusual clarity; as if he had seen them in a film or in a dream and not in real, waking life. Within the hour he would take his own life. And dying, a cut-throat razor in his hand, his blood mingling with the shower-water into the colour of weak wine he would take with him to whatever vacuum lay beyond, three memories: the memory of a green-painted bridge; of an old, bowed, shadowed negro; of the sheer tiled wall of a cubicle in what had originally been the wash-houses of Kensal Rise Tontine and Workingmen's Association, in what was now Kensal Rise Baths.

The extraordinary sense of nervous anticipation the labourer experienced had long been familiar with him. And, inexplicable. He never questioned it fully. He knew he anticipated something, approaching the baths. He knew that it wasn't quite pleasure. It was something more and less than pleasurable, a feeling of ravishing, private vindication, of exposure, of secret, solipsistic victory. Over what he never asked. But he knew. He knew as he approached the baths to wash off the dust of a weeks labour, that this hour would be the week's high-point. Although during the week he never thought of it, never dwelt on its pleasures— as he did, for instance on his prolonged Saturday morning's rest— when the hour came it was as if the secret thread behind his week's existence was emerging into daylight, was exposing itself to the scrutiny of daylight, his daylight. The way the fauna of the sea-bed are exposed, when the tide goes out.

And so when he crossed the marble step at the door, when he faced the lady behind the glass counter, handing her sevenpence, accepting a ticket from her, waving his hand to refuse towel and soap, gesticulating towards the towel in his duffle-bag, each action was performed with the solemnity of an elaborate ritual, each action was a ring in the circular maze that led to the hidden purpose— the purpose he never elaborated, only felt; in his arm as he waved his hand; in his foot as he crossed the threshold. And when he walked down the corridor, with its white walls, its strange hybrid air, half unemployment exchange, half hospital ward, he was silent. As he took his place on the long oak bench, last in a line of negro, Scottish and Irish navvies his expression preserved the same immobility as theirs, his duffle-bag was kept between his feet and his rough slender hands between his knees and his eyes upon the grey cream wall in front of him. He listened to the rich, public voices of the negroes, knowing the warm colours of even their work-clothes without having to look. He listened to the odd mixture of reticence and resentment in the Irish voices. He felt the tiles beneath his feet, saw the flaking wall before him the hard oak bench beneath him, the grey-haired cockney caretaker emerging every now and then from the shower-hall to call 'Shower!', 'Bath!' and at each call the next man in the queue rising, towel and soap under one arm. So plain, so commonplace, and underneath the secret pulsing— but his face was immobile.

As each man left the queue he shifted one space forward and each time the short, crisp call issued from the cockney he turned his head to stare. And when his turn eventually came to be first in the queue and the cockney called 'Shower!' he padded quietly through the open door. He had a slow walk that seemed a little stiff, perhaps because of the unnatural straightness of his back. He had a thin face, unremarkable but for a kind of distance in the expression;

removed, glazed blue eyes; the kind of inwardness there, of immersion, that is sometimes termed stupidity.

The grey-haired cockney took his ticket from him. He nodded towards an open cubicle. The man walked slowly through the rows of white doors, under the tiled roof to the cubicle signified. It was the seventh door down.

'Espera me, Quievo!'.

'Ora, deprisa, ha?'.

He heard splashing water, hissing shower-jets, the smack of palms off wet thighs. Behind each door he knew was a naked man, held timeless and seperate under an umbrella of darting water. The fact of the walls, of the similar but totally seperate beings behind those walls never ceased to amaze him; quietly to excite him. And the shouts of those who communicated echoed strangely through the long, perfectly regular hall. And he knew that everything would be heightened thus now, raised into the aura of the green light.

He walked through the cubicle door and slid the hatch into place behind him. He took in his surroundings with a slow familiar glance. He knew it all but he wanted to be a stranger to it, to see it again for the first time, always the first time: the wall, evenly gridded with white tiles, rising to a height of seven feet; the small gap between it and the ceiling; the steam coming through the gap from the cubicle next door; the jutting wall, with the full-length mirror affixed to it; behind it, enclosed by the plastic curtain, the shower. He went straight to the mirror and stood motionless before it. And the first throes of his removal began to come upon him. He looked at himself

10

the way one would examine a flat-handled trowel, gauging its usefulness; or, idly, the way one would examine the cracks on a city pavement. He watched the way his nostrils, caked with cement-dust, dilated with his breathing. He watched the rise of his chest, the buttons of his soiled white work-shirt straining with each rise, each breath. He clenched his teeth and his fingers. Then he undressed, slowly and deliberately, always remaining in full view of the full-length mirror.

After he was unclothed his frail body with its thin ribs, hard biceps and angular shoulders seemed to speak to him, through its frail passive image in the mirror. He listened and watched.

Later it would speak, lying on the floor with open wrists, still retaining its goose-pimples, to the old cockney shower-attendant and the gathered bathers, every memory behind the transfixed eyes quietly intimated, almost revealed, by the body itself. If they had looked hard enough, had eyes keen enough, they would have known that the skin wouldn't have been so white but for a Dublin childhood, bread and margarine, cramped, carbonated air. The feet with the miniature half-moon scar on the right instep would have told, eloquently, of a summer spent on Laytown Strand, of barefoot walks on a hot beach, of sharded glass and poppies of blood on the summer sand. And the bulge of muscle round the right shoulder would have testified to two years hod-carrying, just as the light, nervous lines across the forehead proclaimed the lessons of an acquisitive metropolis, the glazed eyes themselves demonstrating the failure, the lessons not learnt. All the ill-assorted group of bathers did was

11

pull their towels more rigidly about them, noting the body's glaring pubes, imagining the hair (blonde, maybe) and the skin of the girls that first brought them to life; the first kiss and the indolent smudges of lipstick and all the subsequent kisses, never quite recovering the texture of the first. They saw the body and didn't hear the finer details— just heard that it had been born, had grown and suffered much pain and a little joy; that its dissatisfaction had been deep; and they thought of the green bridge and the red-bricked walls and understood—.

He savoured his isolation for several full minutes. He allowed the cold seep fully through him, after the heat of clothes, sunlight. He saw pale, rising goose-pimples on the mirrored flesh before him. When he was young he had been in the habit of leaving his house and walking down to a busy sea-front road and clambering down from the road to the mud-flats below. The tide would never quite reach the wall and there would be stretches of mud and stone and the long sweep of the cement wall with the five-foot high groove running through it where he could sit, and he would look at the stone, the flat mud and the dried cakes of sea-lettuce and see the tide creep over them and wonder at their impassivity, their imperviousness to feeling; their deadness. It seemed to him the ultimate blessing and he would sit so long that when he came to rise his legs and sometimes his whole body, would be numb. He stood now till his immobility, his cold, became near-agonising. Then he walked slowly to the shower, pulled aside the plastic curtain and walked inside. The tiles had that dead wetness that he had once noticed in the beach-pebbles. He placed each foot squarely on them and saw a thin cake of soap lying in a puddle of grey water. Both were evidence of the bather here before him and he wondered vaguely what he was like; whether he had a quick, rushed shower or a slow, careful one; whether he in turn had wondered about the bather before him. And he stopped wondering, as idly as he had begun. And he turned on the water.

It came hot. He almost cried with the shock of it; a cry of pale, surprised delight. It was a pet love with him, the sudden heat and the wall of water, drumming on his crown, sealing him magically from the world outside; from the universe outside; the pleasurable biting needles of heat; the ripples of water down his hairless arms; the stalactites gathering at each fingertip; wet hair, the sounds of caught breath and thumping water. He loved the pain, the total self-absorption of it and never wondered why he loved it; as with the rest of the weekly ritual— the trudge through the muted officialdom of the bath corridors into the solitude of the shower cubicle, the total ultimate solitude of the boxed, sealed figure, three feet between it and its fellow; the contradictory joy of the first impact of heat, of the pleasurable pain.

An overseer in an asbestos works who had entered his cubicle black and who had emerged with a white, blotchy, greyish skin-hue divined the reason for the cut wrists. He looked at the tiny coagulation of wrinkles round each eye and knew that here was a surfeit of boredom; not a moody, arbitrary, adolescent boredom, but that boredom which is a condition of life itself.

13

He saw the way the mouth was tight and wistful and somehow incommunicative, even in death, and the odour of his first contact with that boredom came back to him. He smelt again the incongruous fish-and-chip smells, the smells of the discarded sweet-wrappings, the metallic odour of the fun-palace, the sulphurous whiff of the dodgem wheels; the empty, musing, poignant smell of the seaside holiday town, for it was here that he had first met his boredom; here that he had wandered the green carpet of the golf-links, with the stretch of grey sky overhead, asking, what to do with the long days and hours, turning then towards the burrows and the long grasses and the strand, deciding there's nothing to do, no point in doing, the sea glimmering to the right of him like the dull metal plate the dodgem wheels ran on. Here he had lain in a sand-bunker for hours, his head making a slight indentation in the sand, gazing at the mordant procession of clouds above. Here he had first asked, what's the point, there's only point if it's fun, it's pleasure, if there's more pleasure than pain; then thinking of the pleasure, weighing up the pleasure in his adolescent scales, the pleasure of the greased fish-and-chip bag warming the fingers, of the sweet taken from the wrapper, the discarded wrapper and the fading sweetness, of the white flash of a pubescent girl's legs, the thoughts of touch and caress, the pain of the impossibility of both and his head digging deeper in the sand he had seen the scales tip in favour of pain. Ever so slightly maybe, but if it wins then what's the point. And he had known the sheep-white clouds scudding through the blueness and

ever after thought of them as significant of the pre-
ponderance of pain; and he looked now at the white
scar on the young man's instep and thought of the
white clouds and thought of the bobbing girls' skirts
and of the fact of pain—.

The first impact had passed; his body temperature
had risen and the hot biting needles were now a
running, massaging hand. And a silence had descended
on him too, after the self immersed orgy of the driving
water. He knew this shower was all things to him, a
world to him. Only here could he see this world, hold
it in balance, so he listened to what was now the
quietness of rain in the cubicle, the hushed, quiet
sound of dripping rain and the green rising mist
through which things are seen in their true, unnatural
clarity. He saw the wet, flapping shower-curtain. There
was a bleak rose-pattern on it, the roses faded by
years of condensation into green: green roses. He saw
the black spaces between the tiles, the plug-hole with
its fading, whorling rivulet of water. He saw the exterior dirt washed off himself, the caked cement-dust,
the flecks of mud. He saw creases of black round his
elbow-joints, a high-water mark round his neck, the
more permanent, ingrained dirt. And he listened to
the falling water, looked at the green roses and wondered what it would be like to see those things, hear
them, doing nothing but see and hear them; nothing
but the pure sound, the sheer colour reaching him; to
be as passive as the mud pebble was to that tide. He
took the cake of soap then from the grilled tray
affixed to the wall and began to rub himself hard.
Soon he would be totally, bleakly clean.

15

There was a dash of paint on his cheek. The negro painter he worked beside had slapped him playfully with his brush. It was disappearing now, under pressure from the soap. And with it went the world, that world, the world he inhabited, the world that left grit under the nails, dust under the eyelids. He scrubbed at the dirt of that world, at the coat of that world, the self that lived in that world, in the silence of the falling water. Soon he would be totally, bleakly clean.

The old cockney took another ticket from another bather he thought he recognised. Must have seen him last week. He crumpled the ticket in his hand, went inside his glass-fronted office and impaled it onto a six-inch nail jammed through a block of wood. He flipped a cigarette from its packet and lit it, wheezing heavily. Long hours spent in the office here, the windows running with condensation, had exaggerated a bronchial condition. He let his eyes scan the seventeen cubicles. He wondered again how many of them, coming every week for seventeen weeks, have visited each of the seventeen showers. None, most likely. Have to go where they're told, don't they. No way they can get into a different box other than the one that's empty, even if they should want to. But what are the chances, a man washing himself ten years here, that he'd do the full round? And the chances that he'd be stuck to the one? He wrinkled his eyes and coughed and rubbed the mist from the window to see more clearly.

White, now. Not the sheer white of the tiles, but a human, flaccid, pink skin-white. He stood upwards, let his arms dangle by his sides, his wrists limp. His short black hair was plastered to his crown like a tight skull-cap. He gazed at the walls of his own cubicle and wondered at the fact that there were sixteen other cubicles around him, identical to this one, which he couldn't see. A man in each, washed by the same water, all in various stages of cleanliness. And he wondered did the form in the next cubicle think of him, his neighbour, as he did. Did he reciprocate his wondering. He thought it somehow appropriate that there should be men naked, washing themselves in adjacent cubicles, each a foreign country to the other. Appropriate to what, he couldn't have said. He looked round his cubicle and wondered: what's it worth, what does it mean, this cubicle— wondered was any one of the other sixteen gazing at his cubicle and thinking, realizing as he was: nothing. He realized that he would never know.

Nothing. Or almost nothing. He looked down at his body: thin belly, thin arms, a limp member. He knew he had arrived at the point where he would mastur-bate. He always came to this point in different ways, with different thoughts, by different stages. But when he had reached it, he always realised that the ways had been similar, the ways had been the same way, only the phrasing different. And he began then, taking him-self with both hands, caressing himself with a familiar, bleak motion, knowing that afterwards the bleakness would only be intensified after the brief distraction of feeling— in this like everything— observing the while the motion of his belly muscles, glistening under their sheen of running water. And as he felt the mechanical surge of desire run through him he heard the splashing of an anonymous body in the cubicle adjacent. The thought came to him that somebody could be watching him. But no, he thought then, almost disappointed, who could, working at himself harder. He was standing when he felt an exultant muscular thrill run through him, arching his back, straining his calves upwards, each toe pressed passionately against the tiled floor.

The young Trinidadian in the next cubicle squeezed out a sachet of lemon soft shampoo and rubbed it to a lather between two brown palms. Flecks of sawdust— he was an apprentice carpenter— mingled with the snow-white foam. He pressed two handfuls of it under each bicep, ladled it across his chest and belly and rubbed it till the foam seethed and melted to the colour of dull whey, and the water swept him clean again, splashed his body back to its miraculous brown and he slapped each nipple laughingly in turn and thought of a clean body under a crisp shirt, of a night of love under a low red-lit roof, of the thumping symmetry of a reggae band.

There was one intense moment of silence. He was standing, spent, sagging. He heard:

'Hey, you rass, not finished yet?'

'How'd I be finished?'

'Well move that corpse, rassman. Move!'

He watched the seed that had spattered the tiles be swept by the shower-water, diluting its grey, ultimately vanishing into the fury of current round the plug-hole. And he remembered the curving cement wall of his childhood and the spent tide and the rocks and the dried green stretches of sea-lettuce and because the exhaustion was delicious now and bleak, because he knew there would never be anything but that exhaustion after all the fury of effort, all the expense of passion and shame, he walked through the green-rose curtain and took the cut-throat razor from his pack and went back to the shower to cut his wrists. And dying, he thought of nothing more significant than the way, the way he had come here, of the green bridge and the bowed figure under the brick wall and the facade of the Victorian bath-house, thinking: there is nothing more significant.

Of the dozen or so people who gathered to stare— as people will— none of them thought: 'Why did he do it?' All of them, pressed into a still, tight circle, staring at the shiplike body, knew intrinsically. And a middle-aged, fat and possibly simple negro phrased the thought:

'Every day the Lord send me I think I do that. And every day the Lord send me I drink bottle of wine and forget 'bout doin that'.

They took with them three memories: the memory of a thin, almost hairless body with reddened wrists; the memory of a thin, finely-wrought razor whose bright silver was mottled in places with rust; and the memory of a spurting shower-nozzle, an irregular drip of water. And when they emerged to the world of bright afternoon streets they saw the green-painted iron bridge and the red-brick wall and knew it to be in the nature of these, too, that the body should act thus—

SEDUCTION

'You don't believe me, do you', he said, 'you don't believe anything, but I've seen her'— and he repeated it again, but I didn't have to listen this time, I could imagine it so vividly. The naked woman's clothes lying in a heap under the drop from the road where the beach was clumsy with rocks and pebbles, her fat body running on the sand at the edge of the water, the waves splashing round her thick ankles. The imagining was just like the whole summer, it throbbed with forbidden promise. I had been back in the town two days and each day we had hung around till twilight, when the hours seemed longest, when the day would extend its dying till it seemed ready to burst, the sky like a piece of stretched gauze over it, grey, melancholy, yet infinitely desirable and unknown. This year I was a little afraid of him, though he was still smaller than me. I envied and loved his pointed shoes that were turned up and scuffed white and his hair that curled and dripped with oil that did its best to contain it in a duck's tail. I loved his assurance, the nonchalant way he let the vinegar run from the chip-bag onto the breast of his off-white shirt. But I kept all this quiet knowing there were things he envied about me too. I think each of us treasured this envy, longing to know how the other had changed but disdaining to ask. We loved to talk in monosyllables conscious of the other's envy, a hidden mutual delight underneath it like blood. Both of us stayed in the same guest-house as last year. My room faced the sea, his the grounds of the convent, the basket-ball pitch with the tennis-net running through it where the nuns swung rackets with brittle, girlish laughter. We sniffed the smell of apples that came over the town from the monastery orchard behind it and the smell of apples in late August meant something different to me this year, as did the twilight. Last year it would have meant an invitation to rob. I wondered did it mean the same to him. I concluded that it must, with his hair like that. But then he was tougher, more obscene.

'Look, she's coming out now'. He nodded his head sideways towards the chip-shop and I stared in through the dripping steamed glass. It looked warm inside, warm and greasy. I saw the woman coming out of the tiny corridor in which the chips were fried, leaning against the steel counter. Some older boys waiting for orders threw jibes at her. She laughed briefly, then took out a cigarette, put it in her mouth and lit it. I knew that when the cigarette came out its tip would

22

be covered in lipstick, the way it happens in films. When she took the coins from them two gold bangles slipped down onto her fat wrist. There was something mysterious, hard and tired about her, some secret behind those layers of make-up which those older boys shared. I watched them laughing and felt the hard excitement of the twilight, the apples. And I believed him then, though I knew how much he lied. I believed him because I wanted to believe it, to imagine it, the nakedness of this fat blonde woman who looked older than her twenty-five years, who sang every Saturday night at the dance in the local hotel.

'Leanche's her name. Leanche the lion'.

'Lioness' I said, being the erudite one. He looked at me and spat.

'When'll you ever dry up'. I spat too. 'Here'. He held out the chip bag.

I took one. It was like when I came to the guesthouse and he had already been there a day. He stood in the driveway pulling leaves off the rhododendron bush as we took things off the rack of our Ford car. I looked over at him, the same as last year, but with a new sullenness in his face. I hoped my face was even more deadpan. He turned his face away when I looked but stayed still, pulling the oily leaves till the unpacking was finished. Then I went over to talk to him. He said that the town was a dump this year, that there was an Elvis playing in the local cinema. He said that Ford cars with high backs had gone out since the ark. I asked him had his people got a car yet and he said no. But somehow it seemed worse to have a car with a high back and rusted doors than no car at all.

He said 'Come on, we'll go to the town' and we both walked to the gate, to the road that ran from the pier towards the town where every house was painted white and yellow and in summer was a guest-house.

'Let's go inside' he said, just as it was getting dark and the last of the queue filed from the chipper. 'We've no money' I said. 'Anyway, I don't believe you'. I hoped my fright didn't glare through. 'It's true', he said. 'The man in the cinema told me'. 'Did he see her' I asked. 'No, his brother did'. There was disdain in the statement that I couldn't have countered.

We pushed open the glass door, he took out a comb as he was doing so and slicked it through his hair. I went over to the yellow jukebox and pushed idly at the buttons. 'Are ye puttin' money in it son'. I heard. I turned and saw her looking at me, the ridiculously small curls of her hair tumbling round her large face. Her cheeks were red and her dress was low and her immense bosom showed white through it, matching the grease-stains on her apron. 'No' I said and began to blush to the roots, 'we just wanted to know . . .'

'Have you got the time' Jamie burst in. 'Have you eyes in your head', she countered. She raised her arm and pointed to a clock in the wall above her. Twenty past ten.

We had walked past the harbour and the chip-shop and the Great Northern Hotel that were all the same as last year. The rich hotelier's son who had left the priesthood and had gone a little mad was on the beach again, turning himself to let his stomach get the sun now that his back was brown. Jamie told me about the two Belfast sisters who wore nylons and who were protestants, how they sat in the cinema every night waiting for something. He asked me had I ever got anything off a girl that wore nylons. I asked him had he. He said nothing, but spat on the ground and stirred the spittle with the sole of his shoe. The difference in the town was bigger now, lurid, hemming us in. I borrowed his comb and slicked it through my hair but my hair refused to quiff, it fell back each time on my forehead, incorrigibly flat and sandy-coloured.

The woman in the chip-shop smiled and crooked her arm on the counter, resting her chin on her fist. The folds of fat bulged round the golden bangles. 'Anything else you'd like to know.' I felt a sudden mad urge to surpass myself, to go one better than Jamie's duck-tailed hair. 'Yeah', I began, 'do you . . . ' Then I stopped. She had seemed a little like an idiot to me but something more than idiocy stopped me. 'Do I!' she said and turned her head towards me, looking at me straight in the eyes. And in the green irises underneath the clumsy mascara there was a mocking light that frightened me. I thought of the moon with a green mist around it like the Angel of Death in the Ten Commandments. I saw her cheeks and heard the wash of the sea and imagined her padding feet on the sand. And I shivered at the deeper, infinite idiocy there, the lurid idiocy that drew couples into long grass to engage in something I wasn't quite sure of. I blushed with shame, with longing to know it, but was saved by her banging hand on the silver counter. 'If you don't want chips, hop it'. 'Don't worry', said Jamie, drawing the comb through his hair. 'Don't worry', I said, listening to his hair click oilily, making for the glass door. 'I still don't believe you', I said to him outside. 'Do you want to wait up and see then'. I didn't answer. Jamie drew a series of curves that formed a naked woman in the window-dew. We both watched them drip slowly into a mess of watery smudges.

We had gone to the cinema that first night, through the yellow-emulsioned doorway into the darkness of the long hall, its windows covered with sheets of brown paper. I smelt the smells of last year, the sweaty felt brass of the seats and the dust rising from the aisle to be changed into diamonds by the cone of light above. There was a scattering of older couples there, there was Elvis on the screen, on a beach in flowered bathing-trunks, but no Belfast sisters. 'Where are they' I asked him, with the ghost of a triumphant note in my voice. He saved himself by taking out a butt, lighting it and pulling harshly on it. We drank in Elvis silently. Later the cinema projectionist put his head between both our shoulders and said 'Hey boys, you want to see the projection-room?' His breath smelt the same as last year, of cigarettes and peppermint. But this year we said no.

Later again I sat in my room and watched the strand, where two nuns were swinging tennis-rackets on a court they had scrawled on the sand. It was ten past nine and the twilight was well advanced, the balance between blue and grey almost perfect. I sat on my bed and pulled my knees to my chest, rocking softly, listening to the nuns' tinkling laughter, staring at the billows their habits made with each swing of their arms. Soon even the nuns left and the strand was empty but for the scrawled tennis-court and the marks of their high-heeled boots. But I watched on, hearing the waves break, letting the light die in the room around me, weeping for the innocence of last year.

We pressed ourselves against the wall below the road, trying to keep our feet from slipping off the large round pebbles. My father was calling my name from the drive of the guest-house. His voice seemed to echo right down the beach, seeming worried and sad. Soon even the echo died away and Jamie clambered up and peeped over the top and waved to me that no-one was there. Then we walked down the strand making a long trail of footsteps in the half-light. We settled ourselves behind an upturned boat and began to wait. We waited for hours, till Jamie's face became pinched and pale, till my teeth began to chatter. He stared at the sea and broke the teeth from his comb, one by one, scattering them at his feet. I spat in the sand and watched how my spittle rolled into tiny sandballs. The sea washed and sucked and washed and sucked but remained empty of fat women. Then Jamie began to talk, about kisses with the mouth open and closed, about the difference between the feel of a breast under and over a jumper, between nylons and short white socks. He talked for what seemed hours and after a while I stopped listening, I knew he was lying anyway. Then suddenly I noticed he had stopped talking. I didn't know how long he had stopped, but I knew had been some time before I noticed it. I turned and saw he was hunched up, his face blank like a child's. All the teeth were broken from his comb, his hand was clutching it insensibly and he was crying softly. His hair was wild with curls, the oil was dripping onto his

27

forehead, his lips were purple with the cold. I touched him on the elbow and when his quiet sobbing didn't stop I took off my coat and put it gingerly round his shoulders. He shivered and moved in close to me and his head touched my chest and lay there. I held him there while he slept, thinking how much smaller than me he was after all.

There was a thin rim of light round the edge of the sea when he woke. His face was pale, and though not as grey as that light, and his teeth had begun to chatter. 'What happened', he asked, shaking my coat off. 'You were asleep' I said, 'you missed it', and began a detailed account of how the woman had begun running from the pier right up past me to the end of the strand, how her breasts had bobbed as the water splashed round her thick ankles. 'Liar' he said. 'Yes' I said. Then I thought of home. 'What are we going to do?' I asked him. He rubbed his eyes with his hand and drew wet smudges across each cheek. Then he got up and began to walk towards the sea. I followed him, knowing the sea would obliterate his tears and any I might have. When he came near the water he began to run, splashing the waves round him with his feet and I ran too, but with less abandon, and when he fell face down in the water I fell too. When I could see him through the salt water he was laughing madly in a crying sort of way, ducking his head in and out of the water the way swimmers do. I got to my feet and tried to pull him up but his clothes were clinging to every bone of his thin body. Then I felt myself slipping, being pulled from the legs and I fell in the water again and I felt his arms around my waist, tightening, the way boys

28

wrestle, but more quietly then, and I felt his body not small any longer, pressing against mine. I heard him say 'this is the way lovers do it' and felt his mouth on my neck but I didn't struggle, I knew that in the water he couldn't see my tears or see my smile.

SAND

The donkey's hooves were like his sister's finger-nails, long and pointed. Except for the ends, which were splintered and rough, not fine and hard.

He was sitting on it, trying to make it move. He could feel its spine against the bone between his legs. He could feel its flanks, like two soft sweaty cushions against each knee and thigh.

He dug his heel into one of the flanks and it shifted a few feet.

'Stop kicking up sand', his sister said. She had that annoyed tone in her voice.

'Will you come for a swim if I stop', he asked.

'Oh just stop, would you'.

'No' he said.

He kicked at the donkey again, though he dreaded his sister's tongue. When she spoke she seemed to

31

know so much that he didn't. It was like her suntan
lotion, like her habit of lying by the sea with her eyes
closed, on their towel. He felt that somewhere he knew
as much as she, but when he came to say it he could
never find the words.

'If you kick more sand at me—'

'Alright', he said. 'Alright'.

He put his hands on the donkey's neck and
wondered how he could get down with some dignity,
some of her dignity. He looked at the dark blue of the
sea and the light blue of the sky, thinking about this.
Then he heard something far away behind him. A
shout. He turned on the donkey, saw someone running
across the burrows, arms waving.

He clambered down quickly, without dignity. He
thought of tinkers. He knew most donkeys belonged to
tinkers. He looked at this donkey and it was as im-
passive as ever, its hooves curling out of the white
sand.

The figure came nearer, running with a peculiar
adult single-mindedness. It wasn't an adult however, it
was a boy, not much older than him. The boy had run
beyond the rim of the grass now and was kicking up
sand. He was totally naked. He held a boot in one hand
with which every now and then he covered his genitals.

But mostly he couldn't cover them, his arms flailing
as he ran. And the boy saw the naked figure, smaller
than him, but stronger and much browner, jogging to
a halt. He saw the open mouth panting and the eyes,
wary as his were, but older and angrier than his could
ever have been. The brown nakedness stopping at the
waist becoming grey-white nakedness. The boot

stationary now in front of the patch of hair.

'That's my donkey. Leave hold of it'.

He did so immediately. Not because he was afraid, which he was, but because he would have done anything those eyes asked. He looked at the shoe and it didn't quite hide that curl of angry hair and that sex. He looked at his sister. She was looking the other way, blushing, arched rigid in her blue swimsuit.

'I'll give you that the next time'.

A small bony fist hovered before his face. Behind it were the eyes, young as his, but with clusters of ancient wrinkles round the edges.

'Okay' he said. He tried not to sound defeated. And the tinker turned and pulled the donkey after him by the thin hair on its neck.

'Really', his sister said.

And now he blushed. The tinker was on the burrows now, pulling the donkey by the hair on it's neck. His buttocks swung as he walked, two white patches against the brown of his thin body.

He felt blamed for that nakedness. He felt he could hate his sister, for blaming him.

'Really', she said. 'Some people'.

He felt the words were false, picked up from grown-ups. Her body was arched forward now towards her drawn-up knees, her arms were placed across her knees and her chin was resting on her arms. Her eyelids were lowered, not quite closed, but sealing him off. He wanted to say sorry, but her eyes lay between him and his words. Then he did hate her. He hated her in a very basic way, he felt he would tear her apart, the way one tears the many wrappings off the parcel in the pass-the-parcel game, to see what's inside. He didn't know whether he'd hate what would be inside.

'Jean—' he began, but she turned on her stomach, away from him, exposing her long back to the sun.

He heard a shout behind him and he turned, glad to escape her. He saw the tinker waving his hands some distance down in the burrows, shouting something he couldn't hear. There was something urgent about him, flailing hands against the sky. So he walked, even though he was afraid, leaving his sister with her cheek resting on her linked hands.

As he walked the tinker grew bigger and the flailing gradually stopped. There was the hot feel of the sand under his bare feet, then the feel of grass, whistling by his calves. Then the boy was in front of him, arms on his hips, waiting for him to approach. He was wearing men's trousers now, sizes too big for him.

'You want a go on the donkey'.

He nodded dumbly.

'I'll give you half an hour with the donkey for half an hour with your sister'.

The boy began to laugh at the thought, his sister and the donkey, an even swop. The tinker began to laugh too and that made the boy laugh louder, huge laughs that went right through his body and stretched his stomach-muscles tight. The tinker's laugh was softer, more knowledgeable. The boy heard this and stopped and looked into the blue eyes which wrinkled in some complicity and kept laughing. Then the boy began to laugh again, loving his laughter, the way he sometimes laughed when adults were laughing. The joke had changed into another joke, a joke he didn't understand, but that made it all the more funny.

Then the tinker stopped suddenly. He cupped his hands together to make a stirrup and held them out.

'Here'.

The hands were grimy and lined, skin flaking off them. The boy felt compliant. He was opening a box to let the winds out. He knew and he didn't know. He placed his left foot in the stirrup of flaking hands and swung onto the donkey and the tinker's foot kicked the donkey and the donkey ran.

He was holding its neck, fearful and exhilarated. It was running like he didn't know donkeys could run with rapid thumps of hoof off the grass, with its spine, hard as a gate, crashing off his groin. He pressed his head against its neck and could hear its breathing, angry and sullen, thumping with its hooves. His knees clutched the swollen belly and his hands, gripping each other under the neck, were wet and slimy with saliva from the open jaw. His eyes were closed and he saw in the black behind his eyelids something even blacker emerging, whorling and retreating again.

Then it stopped. He slid over its head and fell to the ground. He fell flat out, his cheek against the burrows' grass and heard his sister screaming, a clear scream, clear as silver.

The donkey's head was hanging and its sides were heaving. Between its legs a black erection dangled, heaving with its sides. The scream still echoed in the boy's mind. Clear and silver, speaking to him, like the reflection of sun on sea-water. He ran.

He ran faster than the donkey. He saw the green burrows, then the white sand, then the clear blue of his sister's swimsuit then a browned tanned back. The sand was kicking up in clumps around him as he threw himself on that back.

He felt the naked shoulders under his hand. Then he felt the shoulders twisting and a hard body pushing him downwards, something hot, hard against his stomach. Both of their fists were hitting the other's face until he was hit hard, once and twice and they both, as if by mutual decision, went quiet. He lay until he became conscious of the other's hot hard groin, then squirmed away. He looked up at his sister. Her head was in one hand and the other hand was covering the bare skin above her swimsuit. He heard a rustle of sand and heard the tinker boy getting up.

'I thought we'd made a swop'. There was a spot of blood on his wizened mouth. He bent forward as if to strike again but changed his hand's direction just as rapidly and scratched the hair behind his ear. The boy started. He grinned.

'I'd only put it through you' he said. Then he hitched up his falling trousers and walked towards the grass.

When he got there he turned.

'That's the last you'll see of my dunkey', he said. Then he chuckled with infinite sarcasm. 'Unless you've got another sister'. And he turned again and walked through the grass towards the donkey.

She was crying, great breathful sobs.

'You won't—', he asked.

'I will', she said. 'I'll tell it all—'

The boy knew, however, that she would be ashamed. He picked up her towel and her suntan lotion and began to walk. He had forgotten about his hate. He was thinking of the donkey and the tinker's flaking palms and his sister's breasts. After a while he turned.

'Stop crying, will you. Nothing happened, did it.'

His hands were wet with the donkey's saliva and to the saliva a fine film of sand was clinging. When he moved his fingers it rustled, whispered, sang.

MR SOLOMON WEPT

The child had rolled pennies and the dodgem wheels had smoked for half a morning when Mr Solomon took time off to stand by the strand. He stood where he was accustomed to, on the lip of the cement path that seemed designed to run right to the sea but that crumbled suddenly and inexplicably into the sand. Mr Solomon smoked a cigarette there, holding it flatly between his lips, letting the smoke drift over his thin moustache into his nostrils. His eyes rested on the lumps of rough-cast concrete half-embedded in the sand. His breath came in with a soft, scraping sound.

The sea looked warm and lazy in midday. Down the beach a marquee was being erected. Mr Solomon looked at the people on the beach, the sunbathers and the men who were unwinding the marquee canvas. He wore a brown suit with narrow legs and wide lapels, his thin face looked like it was long accustomed to viewing sunbathers, people on beaches. Mr Solomon then stopped looking at the people and looked at the sea. He took the cigarette from his mouth, inhaled and replaced it again. The sea looked dark blue to him, the colour of midnight rather than of midday. And though it looked flat and indolent and hot, its blueness was clear and sharp, a sharpness emphasised by the occasional flurry of white foam, the slight swell far out. Mr Solomon knew these to be white horses. But today they reminded him of lace, lace he imagined round a woman's throat, a swelling bosom underneath, covered in navy cloth. He had seen an advertisement for Sherry once with such a picture. He saw her just under the sea, just beneath the film of glassblue. If he lifted his eyes to the horizon again the sea became flat and indolent, and probably too hot for swimming.

Mr Solomon lifted his eyes and saw the flat sea and the flat yellow strand. He thought of the child he had left, something morose and forlorn about the way he pushed penny after penny into the metal slot. Then he looked down the strand and saw the large marquee pole being hoisted and only then realised that it was race day. And Mr Solomon remembered the note again, he remembered the nights of surprised pain, the odd gradual feeling of deadness, how before it happened it had been unthinkable and how after it happened somehow anything other than it had become unthinkable. Now he dressed the boy, shopped, the boy sat in the change booth staring at the racing page while he drank in the Northern Star over lunchtime. He remembered how his wife had left him on Race day, one year ago. How he had come to Laytown three days before the races, to catch the crowds. How on the fourth day he had gone to the caravan behind the rifle-range and found it empty, a note on the flap table. It's message was hardly legible, though simple. Gone with Chas. Won't have to hate you any more. He remembered how he had wondered who Chas was, how he had sat on the unmade bed and stared at this note that over the length of the first night assumed the significance of a train ticket into a country he had never heard of. For he had long ceased to think of her with the words love or hate, he had worked, rolled his thin cigarettes, she had totted the books while he supervised the rent, those words were like the words school or god, part of a message that wasn't important any more, a land that was far away. And now he saw the note and thought of the world that had lived for her, thought of the second May, the May behind the one that woke first beside him in the cramped white caravan, that was sitting beside the singing kettle when he woke; this was Chas's May— but it mightn't have been Chas, it could have spelt Chad— and the thought that she existed gave him a feeling of surprised pain, surprise at the May he had never known of, surprise at the loss of what he had never possessed. But after three days the pained surprise had died and a new surprise asserted itself— a surprise at how easily the unthinkable became possible. He found it was easy to cook, to tot the books, to supervise the dodgem tracks and shooting-range all in one. The boy helped him, he watched the boy from behind the glass of the change booth emptying the slot-machines. When the races finished he stayed on, found

40

the move to another holiday-spot too much bother and unnecessary anyway, since less money would do now. Even when the season ended he didn't move, he sat in the draughty amusement hall through winter and made more than enough to keep rolling his thin cigarettes. The rusted slot-machines became a focus for the local youths with sullen faces and greased hair and he found forgetting her almost as easy a task as that of living with her had been. She had been shrewish, he told himself as her memory grew dimmer, her hair had often remained unwashed for days, she would have soon, within the year, gone too fat. Thus he killed the memory of another her neatly, he forgot the nights at the Palais in Brighton, the evenings in the holiday pubs, her platinum hair and the rich dark of the bottled Guinness (a ladies drink then) tilted towards her laughing mouth.

But he saw the marquee pole stagger upright and suddenly remembered her as if she had died and as if the day of the Laytown Races was her anniversary. He saw the white horses whip and the marquee canvas billow round the pole and thought suddenly of the dress she had called her one good dress with its sad lace frills and the bodice of blue satin that had more restitchings than original threads. A sense of grief came over him, a feeling of quiet sadness, not wholly un-pleasing. He began to think of her as if she had died, he thought of the woman who had lived with him and who indeed had died. He imagined flowers for her, dark blood-red roses and felt bleak and clean as if in celebration of her imagined death he was somehow cleansing both him and his image of her.

He lit another cigarette and turned back on the cement path. He passed a family coming from an ice-cream van a little down it, the cones in their hands already sodden. Mr Solomon watched them pass him and felt he had a secret safe, totally safe from them. He felt as if there was a hidden flame inside him, consuming him, while the exterior remained the same as ever, the smoke still drifted over the same thin lip. He passed the green corrugated hall that served as a golf-club and remembered how each year they came through she had got him to pay green fees, how they had both made an afternoon's slow crawl over nine holes. How she had longed to be someday, a proper member in a proper club. 'But we never settle down enough, do we Jimmy, 'cept in winter, when it's too wet to play . . .'

Mr Solomon walked down the cement walk away from the beach and the rising marquee and felt his grief inside him like old port, hot and mellow. He came to the tarmac road and stood, staring at the tottering facade of the amusements and the dull concrete front of the Northern Star opposite. He wavered for one moment and then headed for the brass-studded door of the Northern Star, the mute lights and wood-and-brass fittings being like night to him at first until his eyes settled. He ordered a drink and gave the barman a sharp look before downing it.

'This one's for my wife', he said.

'I didn't know you had one' said the barman, who was always courteous.

'In memory of her. She died last year'.

'I'm sorry', said the barman. 'Her anniversary?'

'Died on race day', began Mr Solomon but by this time the barman had headed off discreetly for a customer at the other end. He blinked once then finished his drink and began to feel very angry at the courteous barman. He felt the whiskey tickle down his throat, he felt something in him had been sullied by the bland courtesy, the discreet lights of the hotel bar. He left.

Outside the brightness blinded him as much as the darkness had before. Mr Solomon stared down the lean yellow street. It was packed with people and as he watched them, Mr Solomon began to feel for the first time a hatred towards them, en masse. He felt a malignant sameness in them. He felt they laughed, in their summer clothes. He felt they didn't know, in their summer clothes. He felt like a cog in the mechanism of holidays, of holiday towns, he felt somehow slave to their bright clothes and suntans. He no longer felt she had died, he felt something had killed her, that impersonal holiday gaiety had enslaved them both, had aged him, like a slow cancerous growth, had annihilated her. He felt his grief burning inside now, like a rough Irish whiskey. He crossed the street a little faster than he normally did, though his walk was still lethargic by the street's standards. He went into the pub with the black-and-white gabled roof.

That afternoon his tale competed with the banjo-playing tinker, with the crack of beer-glasses, with the story of the roadworker's son who returned and bought out three local publicans. Mr Solomon shouted it, wept it, crowed with it, nobody listened, his thin face acquired a weasel look, a sorry look, his eyes grew more glazed and his speech more blurred, the reason for his grief grew hazy and indeterminate. By half-past four he was just drunk, all he knew was there was something somewhere to feel sorry over, profoundly sorry, somewhere a pain, though the reason for it he could no longer fathom, nor why it should be his pain particularly. Why not that Meath farmer's, with the flushed face and the tweed suit, and at this Mr Solomon grew offensive, sloppily offensive and found himself removed.

He went through the hard daylight again into the dark of the Amusement Parlour. He heard a rustle in the left-hand corner and saw the boy starting up guiltily from the peepshow machine. Mr Solomon thought of the near-naked starlets in high-heels and out-of-date hairdos and got angry again. 'I told you never to go near that', he rasped. The boy replied with a swift obscenity that shocked him silent. He could only stare, at his homemade cloth anorak, his hair clumsily quiffed, sticking out in places, his thin impenetrable face. At his son's face, new to him because he'd never seen it. He made to move towards him, only then realising how drunk he was. He saw the boy's hand draw back and an object fly from it. He raised his hand to protect his face and felt something strike his knuckles. He heard the coin ring off the cement floor and the boy's footsteps running towards the door. He ran after him drunkenly, shouting.

The boy ran towards the beach. Mr Solomon followed. He saw the horses thunder on the beach, distorted by his drunken run. He saw the line of sand they churned up, the sheets of spray they raised when they galloped in the tide. He saw the boy running for the marquee.

Mr Solomon could hear a brass band playing. He ran till he could run no longer and then he went forward in large clumsy steps, dragging the sand as he went. The sound of the reeds and trumpets grew clearer as he walked, repeated in one poignant phrase, right down the beach. Mr Solomon came to a crowd then, pressed round the marquee and began to push his way desperately through it. He felt people like a wall against him, forcing him out. He began to moan aloud, scrabbling at the people in front of him to force his way in. He imagined the boy at the centre of that crowd, playing a clear golden trumpet. He could see the precise curve of the trumpet's mouth, the pumping keys, the boy's expressionless eyes. He began to curse, trying to wedge himself between the bodies, there was something desperate and necessary beyond them.

He felt himself lifted then, carried a small distance off and thrown in the sand. He lifted his face and wept in the sand and saw the horses churning the sea-spray into a wide area down by the edge. He heard a loud cheer, somewhere behind him.

NIGHT IN TUNISIA

That year they took the green house again. She was there again, older than him and a lot more venal. He saw her on the white chairs that faced the tennis-court and again in the burrows behind the tennis-court and again still down on the fifteenth hole where the golf-course met the mouth of the Boyne. It was twilight each time he saw her and the peculiar light seemed to suspend her for an infinity, a suspended infinite silence, full of years somehow. She must have been seventeen now that he was fourteen. She was fatter, something of an exhausted woman about her and still something of the girl whom adults called mindless. It was as if a cigarette between her fingers had burnt towards the tip without her noticing. He heard people talking about her even on her first day there, he learnt that underneath her frayed blouse her wrists were marked.

She was a girl about whom they would talk anyway since she lived with a father who drank, who was away for long stretches in England. Since she lived in a green corrugated-iron house. Not even a house, a chalet really, like the ones the townspeople built to house summer visitors. But she lived in it all the year round.

They took a green house too that summer, also made of corrugated iron. They took it for two months this time, since his father was playing what he said would be his last stint, since there was no more place for brassmen like him in the world of three-chord showbands. And this time the two small bedrooms were divided differently, his sister taking the small one, since she had to dress on her own now, himself and his father sharing the larger one where two years ago his sister and he had slept. Every night his father took the tenor sax and left for Mosney to play with sixteen others for older couples who remembered what the big bands of the forties sounded like. And he was left alone with his sister who talked less and less as her breasts grew bigger. With the alto saxaphone which his father said he could learn when he forgot his fascination for three-chord ditties. With the guitar which he played a lot, as if in spite against the alto saxaphone. And with the broken-keyed piano which he played occasionally.

48

When it rained on the iron roof the house sang and he was reminded of a green tin drum he used to hand when he was younger. It was as if he was inside it.

He wandered round the first three days, his sister formal and correct beside him. There was one road made of tarmac, running through all the corrugated houses towards the tennis-court. It was covered always with drifts of sand, which billowed while they walked. They passed her once, on the same side, like an exotic and dishevelled bird, her long yellow cardigan coming down to her knees, covering her dress, if she wore any. He stopped as she passed and turned to face her. Her feet kept billowing up the sand, her eyes didn't see him, they were puffy and covered in black pencil. He felt hurt. He remembered an afternoon three years ago when they had lain on the golf links, the heat, the nakedness that didn't know itself, the grass on their three backs.

'Why don't you stop her?' he asked his sister.

'Because', she answered. 'Because, because'.

He became obsessed with twilights. Between the hour after tea when his father left and the hour long after dark when his father came home he would wait for them, observe them, he would taste them as he would a sacrament. The tincture of the light fading, the blue that seemed to be sucked into a thin line beyond the sea into what the maths books called infinity, the darkness falling like a stone. He would look at the long shadows of the burrows on the strand and the long shadows of the posts that held the sagging tennis-nets on the tarmac courts. He would watch his sister walking down the road under the eyes of boys that were a little older than him. And since he hung around at twilight and well into the dark he came to stand with them, on the greens behind the clubhouse, their cigarette-tips and their laughter punctuating the dark. He played all the hits on the honky-tonk piano in the clubhouse for them and this compensated for his missing years. He played and he watched, afraid to say too much, listening to their jokes and their talk about girls, becoming most venal when it centred on her.

He laughed with them, that special thin laugh that can be stopped as soon as it's begun.

There was a raft they would swim out to on the beach. His skin was light and his arms were thin and he had no Adam's apple to speak of, no hair creeping over his togs, but he would undress all the same with them and swim out. They would spend a day on it while the sun browned their backs and coaxed beads of resin from the planks. When they shifted too much splinters of wood shot through their flesh. So mostly they lay inert, on their stomachs, their occasional erections hidden beneath them, watching on the strand the parade of life.

It galled his father what he played.

'What galls me', he would say, 'is that you could be so good'.

But he felt vengeful and played them incessantly and even sang the tawdry lyrics. Some day soon, he sang, I'm going to tell the Moon about the crying game. And maybe he'll explain, he sang.

'Why don't you speak to her?' he asked his sister when they passed her again. It was seven o'clock and it was getting dark.

'Because' she said. 'Because I don't'.

But he turned. He saw her down the road, her yellow cardigan making a scallop round her fattening buttocks.

'Rita', he called. 'Rita'.

She turned. She looked at him blankly for a moment and then she smiled, her large pouting lips curving the invitation she gave to any boy that shouted at her.

He sat at the broken-keyed piano. The light was going down over the golf-links and his sister's paper-back novel was turned over on the wooden table. He heard her in her room, her shoes knocking off the thin wooden partition. He heard the rustling of cotton and nylon and when the rustles stopped for a moment he got up quickly from the piano and opened the door. She gave a gasp and pulled the dress from the pile at her feet to cover herself. He asked her again did she remember and she said she didn't and her face blushed with such shame that he felt sorry and closed the door again.

The sea had the movement of cloth but the texture of glass. It flowed and undulated, but shone hard and bright. He thought of cloth and glass and how to mix them. A cloth made of glass fibre or a million woven mirrors. He saw that the light of twilight was repeated or reversed at early morning.

He decided to forget about his sister and join them,

the brashness they were learning, coming over the transistors, the music that cemented it. And the odd melancholy of the adulthood they were about to straddle, to ride like a Honda down a road with one white line, pointless and inevitable.

His father on his nights off took out his Selmer, old loved talisman that was even more shining than on the day he bought it. He would sit and accompany while his father stood and played— 'That Certain Feeling', 'All The Things You Are', the names that carried their age with them, the embellishments and the filled-in notes that must have been something one day but that he had played too often, that he was too old now to get out of. And to please his father he would close his eyes and play, not knowing how or what he played and his father would stop and let him play on, listening. And he would occasionally look and catch that look in his listening eyes, wry, sad and loving, his pleasure at how his son played only marred by the knowledge of how little it meant to him. And he would catch the look in his father's eyes and get annoyed and deliberately hit a bum note to spoil it. And the sadness in the eyes would outshine the wryness then and he would be sorry, but never sorry enough.

He soon learnt that they were as mistrustful of each other as he was of them and so he relaxed somewhat. He learnt to turn his silence into a pose. They listened to his playing and asked about his sister. They lay on the raft, watched women on the strand, their eyes stared so hard that the many shapes on the beach became one, indivisible. It made the sand-dunes and even the empty clubhouse redundant. Lying face down on the warm planks, the sun burning their backs with an aching langour. The blaring transistor, carried over in its plastic bag. Her on the beach, indivisible, her yellow cardigan glaring even on the hottest days. He noticed she had got fatter since he came. Under them on the warm planks the violent motions of their pricks. She who lived in the chalet all the year round.

The one bedroom and the two beds, his father's by the door, his by the window. The rippled metal walls. The moon like water on his hands, the bed beside him empty. Then the front door opening, the sound of the saxaphone case lied down. His eyes closed, his father stripping in the darkness, climbing in, long underwear and vest. The body he'd known lifelong, old and somewhat loved, but not like his Selmer, shining. They get better with age, he said about instruments. His breath scraping the air now, scraping over the wash of the sea, sleeping.

The tall thin boy put his mouth to the mouth of the french letter and blew. It expanded, huge and bulbous, with a tiny bubble at the tip.

'It's getting worked up', he said.

He had dark curling hair and dark shaven cheeks and a mass of tiny pimples where he shaved. The pimples spread from his ears downwards, as if scattered from a pepper-canister. His eyes were dark too, and always a little closed.

'We'll let it float to England', he said, 'so it can find a fanny big enough for it'.

They watched it bobbing on the waves, brought back and forwards with the wash. Then a gust of wind lifted it and carried it off, falling to skim the surface and rising again, the bubble towards the sky.

He had walked up from the beach and the french letter bound for England. He had seen her yellow cardigan on the tennis-court from a long way off, above the strand. He was watching her play now, sitting on the white wrought-iron seat, his hands be-tween his legs.

She was standing on the one spot, dead-centre of the court, hardly looking at all at her opponent. She was hitting every ball cleanly and lazily and the sound that came from her racquet each time was that taut twang that he knew only came from a good shot. He felt that even a complete stranger would have known, from her boredom, her ease, that she lived in a holiday town with a tennis-court all the year round. The only sign of effort was the beads of sweat round her lips and the tousled blonde curls round her forehead. And every now and then when the man she was playing against managed to send a shot towards the sidelines, she didn't bother to follow it at all. She let the white ball bounce impotent towards the wire mesh.

He watched the small fat man he didn't recognise lose three balls for every ball won. He relished the spectacle of a fat man in whites being beaten by a bored teenage girl in sagging high-heels. Then he saw her throw her eyes upwards, throw her racquet down and walk from the court. The white ball rolled towards the wire mesh.

She sat beside him. She didn't look at him but she spoke as if she had known him those three years.

'You play him. I'm sick of it'.

He walked across the court and his body seemed to glow with the heat generated by the slight touch of hers. He picked up the racquet and the ball, placed his foot behind the white line and threw the ball up, his eye on it, white, skewered against the blue sky. Then it came down and he heard the resonant twang as his racquet hit it and it went spinning into the opposite court but there was no-one there to take it. He looked up and saw the fat man and her walking towards a small white car. The fat man gestured her in and she looked behind at him once before she entered.

And as the car sped off towards Mornington he swore she waved.

The car was gone down the Mornington road. He could hear the pop-pop of the tennis-balls hitting the courts and the twang of them hitting the racquets as he walked, growing fainter. He walked along the road, past the tarmac courts and past the grass courts and past the first few holes of the golf-course which angled in a T round the tennis courts. He walked past several squares of garden until he came to his. It wasn't really a garden, a square of sand and scutch. He walked through the gate and up the path where the sand had been trodden hard to the green corrugated door. He turned the handle in the door, always left open. He saw the small square room, the sand fanning across the line from the doorstep, the piano with the sheet-music perched on the keys. He thought of the midday sun outside, the car with her in the passenger seat moving through it, the shoulders of the figure in the driver's seat. The shoulders hunched and fat, expressing something venal. He thought of the court, the white tennis ball looping between her body and his. Her body relaxed, vacant and easeful, moving the racquet so the ball flew where she wished. His body worried, worrying the whole court. He felt there was something wrong, the obedient ball, the running man. What had she lost to gain that ease, he wondered. He thought of all the jokes he had heard and of the act behind the jokes that none of those who told the jokes experienced. The innuendos and the charged words like the notes his father played, like the melodies his father willed him to play. The rich full twang as the ball met her racquet at the centre.

He saw the alto saxaphone on top of the piano. He took it down, placed it on the table and opened the case. He looked at the keys, remembering the first lessons his father had taught him when it was new-bought, months ago. The keys unpressed, mother-of-pearl on gold, spotted with dust. He took out the ligature and fixed the reed in the mouthpiece. He put it between his lips, settled his fingers and blew. The note came out harsh and childish, as if he'd never learnt. He heard a shifting movement in the inside room and knew that he'd woken his father.

He put the instrument back quickly and made for the tiny bathroom. He closed the door behind him quietly, imagining his father's grey vest rising from the bed to the light of the afternoon sun. He looked into the mirror that closed on the cabinet where the medicine things were kept. He saw his face in the mirror looking at him, frightened, quick glance. Then he saw his face taking courage and looking at him full-on, the brown eyes and the thin fragile jawline. And he began to look at his eyes as directly as they looked at him.

'You were playing', his father said, in the livingroom, in shirtsleeves, in uncombed afternoon hair, 'the alto—'

'No', he said, going for the front door, 'you were dreaming—'.

And on the raft the fat asthmatic boy, obsessed more than any with the theatre on the strand, talking about 'it' in his lisping, mournful voice, smoking cigarettes that made his breath wheeze more. He had made classifications, rigid as calculus, meticulous as algebra. There were girls, he said, and women, and in between them what he termed lady, the lines of de-marcation finely and inexorably drawn. Lady was thin and sat on towels, with high-heels and suntan-lotions, without kids. Woman was fat, with rugs and breasts that hung or bulged, with children. Then there were girls, his age, thin, fat and middling, nyloned, short-stockinged—

He lay on his stomach on the warm wood and listened to the fat boy talking and saw her walking down the strand. The straggling, uncaring walk that, he decided, was none of these or all of these at once. She was wearing flat shoes that went down at the heels with no stockings and the familiar cardigan that hid what could have classified her. She walked to a spot up the beach from the raft and unrolled the bundled towel from under her arm. Then she kicked off her shoes and pulled off her cardigan and wriggled out of the skirt her cardigan had hidden. She lay back on the towel in the yellow bathing suit that was too young for her, through which her body seemed to press like a butterfly already moulting in its chrysalis. She took a bottle then and shook it into her palm and began rubbing the liquid over her slack exposed body.

He listened to the fat boy talking about her— he was local too— about her father who on his stretches home came back drunk and bounced rocks off the tin roof, shouting 'Hewer'.

'What does that mean', he asked.

'Just that', said the asthmatic boy. 'Rhymes with sure'.

He looked at her again from the raft, her slack stomach bent forward, her head on her knees. He saw her head lift and turn lazily towards the raft and he stood up then, stretching his body upwards, under what he imagined was her gaze. He dived, his body imagining itself suspended in air before it hit the water. Underwater he held his breath, swam through the flux of tiny bubbles, like crotchets before his open eyes.

'What did you say she was', he asked the fat boy, swimming back to the raft.

'Hewer', said the fat boy, more loudly.

He looked towards the strand and saw her on her back, her slightly plump thighs towards the sky, her hands shielding her eyes. He swam to the side of the raft then and gripped the wood with one hand and the fat boy's ankle with the other and pulled. The fat boy came crashing into the water and went down and when his head came up, gasping for asthmatic breath, he forced it down once more, though he didn't know what whore meant.

His father was cleaning the alto when he came back.

'What does hewer mean', he asked his father.

His father stopped screwing in the ligature and looked at him, his old sideman's eyes surprised, and somewhat moral.

'A woman', he said, 'who sells her body for monetary gain'.

He stopped for a moment. He didn't understand.

'That's tautology', he said.

'What's that?' his father asked.

'It repeats', he said, and went into the toilet.

He heard the radio crackle over the sound of falling

61

water and heard a rapid-fire succession of notes that
seemed to spring from the falling water, that amazed
him, so much faster than his father ever played, but
slow behind it all, melancholy, like a river. He came
out of the toilet and stood listening with his father.
Who is that, he asked his father. Then he heard the
continuity announcer say the name Charlie Parker and
saw his father staring at some point between the
wooden table and the wooden holiday-home floor.

He played later on the piano in the clubhouse with
the dud notes, all the songs, the trivial mythologies
whose significance he had never questioned. It was as if
he was fingering through his years and as he played he
began to forget the melodies of all those goodbyes and
heartaches, letting his fingers take him where they
wanted to, trying to imitate that sound like a river he
had just heard. It had got dark without him noticing
and when finally he could just see the keys as question-
marks in the dark, he stopped. He heard a noise behind
him, the noise of somebody who has been listening,
but who doesn't want you to know they are there. He
turned and saw her looking at him, black in the square
of light coming through the door. Her eyes were on his
hands that were still pressing the keys and there was a
harmonic hum tiny somewhere in the air. Her eyes rose
to his face, unseeing and brittle to meet his hot, tense
stare. He still remembered the rough feel of the tartan
blanket over them, three of them, the grass under

62

them. But her eyes didn't, so he looked everywhere but on them, on her small pinched chin, ridiculous under her large face, on the yellow linen dress that was ragged round her throat, on her legs, almost black from so much sun. The tiny hairs on them glistened with the light behind her. He looked up then and her eyes were still on his, keeping his fingers on the keys, keeping the chord from fading.

He was out on the burrows once more, he didn't know how, and he met the thin boy. The thin boy sat down with him where they couldn't be seen and took a condom from his pocket and masturbated among the bushes. He saw how the liquid was caught by the anti-septic web, how the sand clung to it when the thin boy threw it, like it does to spittle.

He left the thin boy and walked down the beach, empty now of its glistening bodies. He looked up at the sky, from which the light was fading, like a thin silver wire. He came to where the beach faded into the mouth of a river. There was a statue there, a Virgin with thin fingers towards the sea, her feet layered with barnacles. There were fishermen looping a net round the mouth. He could see the dim line of the net they pulled and the occasional flashes of white salmon. And as the boat pulled the net towards the shore he saw how the water grew violent with flashes, how the loose shoal of silver-and-white turned into a panting, open-gilled pile. He saw the net close then, the fishermen lifting it, the water falling from it, the salmon laid bare, glutinous, clinging, wet, a little like boiled rice.

He imagined the glistening bodies that littered the beach pulled into a net like that. He imagined her among them, slapping for space, panting for air, he heard transistors blare Da Doo Run Run, he saw sun-tan-lotion bottles crack and splinter as the Fisher up above pulled harder. He imagined his face like a life-guard's, dark sidelocks round his muscular jaw, a megaphone swinging from his neck, that crackled.

He saw the thin band of light had gone, just a glow off the sea now. He felt frightened, but forced himself not to run. He walked in quick rigid steps past the bar-nacled Virgin then and down the strand.

'Ten bob for a touch with the clothes on. A pound without'.

They were playing pontoon on the raft. He was watching the beach, the bodies thicker than salmon. When he heard the phrase he got up and kicked the dirt-cards into the water. He saw the Queen of Hearts face upwards in the foam. As they made for him he dived and swam out a few strokes.

'Cunts', he yelled from the water. 'Cunts'.

On the beach the wind blew fine dry sand along the surface, drawing it in currents, a tide of sand.

His sister laid the cups out on the table and his father ate with long pauses between mouthfuls. His father's hand paused, the bread quivering in the air, as if he were about to say something. He looked at his sister's breasts across a bowl of apples, half-grown fruits. The apples came from monks who kept an orchard. Across the fields, behind the house. He imagined a monk's hand reaching for the unplucked fruit, white against the swinging brown habit. For monks never sunbathed.

When he had finished he got up from the table and idly pressed a few notes on the piano.

'Why do you play that', his father asked. He was still at the table, between mouthfuls.

'I don't know', he said.

'What galls me', said his father, 'is that you could be good'.

He played a bit more of the idiotic tune that he didn't know why he played.

'If you'd let me teach you', his father said, 'you'd be glad later on'.

'Then why not wait till later on and teach me then'.

'Because you're young, you're at the age. You'll never learn as well as now, if you let me teach you. You'll never feel things like you do now'.

He began to play again in defiance and then stopped.

'I'll pay you', his father said.

His father woke him coming in around four. He heard his wheezing breath and his shuffling feet. He watched the grey, metal-coloured light filling the room that last night had emptied it. He thought of his father's promise to pay him. He thought of the women who sold their bodies for monetary gain. He imagined all of them on the dawn golf-course, waking in their dew-sodden clothes. He imagined fairways full of them, their monetary bodies covered with fine drops of water. Their dawn chatter like birdsong. Where was that golf-course, he wondered. He crept out of bed and into his clothes and out of the door, very quietly. He crossed the road and clambered over the wire fence that separated the road from the golf-course. He walked through several fairways, across several greens, past several fluttering pennants with the conceit in his mind all the time of her on one green, asleep and sodden, several pound notes in her closed fist. At the fourteenth green he then saw that the dull metal colour had faded into morning, true morning. He began to walk back, his feet sodden from the dew.

He went in through the green corrugated door and put on a record of the man whose playing he had first heard two days ago. The man played 'Night in Tunisia', and the web of notes replaced the web that had tightened round his crown. The notes soared and fell, dispelling the world around him, tracing a series of arcs that seemed to point to a place, or if not a place, a state of mind. He closed his eyes and let the music fill him and tried to see that place. He could see a landscape of small hills, stretching to infinity, suffused in a yellow light that seemed to lap like water. He decided it was a place you were always in, yet always trying to reach, you walked towards all the time and yet never got there, as it was always beside you. He opened his eyes and wondered where Tunisia was on the Atlas. Then he stopped wondering and reached up to the piano and took down the alto saxophone and placed it on the table. He opened the case and saw it gleaming in the light, new and unplayed. He knew he was waking his father from the only sleep he ever got, but he didn't care, imagining his father's pleasure. He heard him moving in the bedroom then, and saw him come in, his hair dishevelled, putting his shirt on. His father sat then, while he stood, listening to the sounds that had dispelled the world. When it had finished his father turned down the volume controls and took his fingers and placed them on the right keys and told him to blow.

He learned the first four keys that day and when his father took his own instrument and went out to his work in Butlins he worked out several more for himself. When his father came back, at two in the morning, he was still playing. He passed him in the room, neither said anything, but he could feel his father's pleasure, tangible, cogent. He played on while his father undressed in the bedroom and when he was asleep he put it down and walked out the door, across the hillocks of the golf-course onto the strand, still humid with the warmth of that incredible summer.

He forgot the raft and the games of pontoon and the thin boy's jargon. He stayed inside for days and laboriously transferred every combination of notes he had known on the piano onto the metal keys. He lost his tan and the gold sheen of the instrument became quickly tarnished with sweat, the sweat that came off his fingers in the hot metal room. He fashioned his mouth round the reed till the sounds he made became like a power of speech, a speech that his mouth was the vehicle for but that sprang from the knot of his stomach, the crook of his legs.

As he played he heard voices and sometimes the door knocked. But he turned his back on the open window and the view of the golf-course. Somewhere, he thought, there's a golf-course where bodies are free, not for monetary gain—

He broke his habit twice. Once he walked across the fields to the orchard where the monks plucked fruit with white fingers. He sat on a crumbling wall and watched the darkening and fading shadows of the apple trees. Another night he walked back down the strand to where it faded into the river mouth. He looked at the salmonless water and imagined the life-guard up above calling through his megaphone. He imagined childhood falling from him, coming off his palms like scales from a fish. He didn't look up, he looked down at his fingers that were forming hard coats of skin at the tips, where they touched the keys.

And then, ten days after it had started, his face in the mirror looked older to him, his skin paler, his chin more ragged, less round. His father got up at half-past three and played the opening bars of 'Embraceable You' and instead of filling in while his father played, he played while his father filled in. And then they both played, rapidly, in a kind of mutual anger, through all his favourites into that area where there are no tunes, only patterns like water, that shift and never settle.

And his father put his instrument away and put several pound notes on the table. He took them, put the case up above the piano and went out the green door.

It was five o'clock as he walked down the road by the golf-course, squinting in the sunlight. He walked down by the tennis-court onto the strand, but it was too late now and the beach was empty and there was no-one on the raft.

He walked back with the pound notes hot in his pocket and met the fat boy with two racquets under his arm. The fat boy asked him did he want to play and he said 'Yes'.

They had lobbed an endless series of balls when the fat boy said 'Did you hear?' 'Hear what', he asked and then the fat boy mentioned her name. He told him how the lifeguard had rescued her twice during the week, from a part of the beach too near the shore to drown in by accident. He hit the ball towards the fat boy and imagined her body in the lifeguard's arms, his mouth on her mouth, pushing the breath in. Then

71

he saw her sitting on the iron-wrought seat in a green dress now, vivid against the white metal. The pound notes throbbed in his pocket, but he hadn't the courage to stop playing and go to the seat. Her eyes were following the ball as it went backwards and forwards, listless and vacant. The light gradually became grey, almost as grey as the ball, so in the end he could only tell where it fell by the sound and they missed more than half the volleys. But still she sat on the white chair, her eyes on the ball, following it forwards and back. He felt a surge of hope in himself. He would tell her about that place, he told himself, she doesn't know. When it got totally dark he would stop, he told himself, go to her. But he knew that it never gets totally dark and he just might never stop and she might never rise from the white seat.

He hit the ball way above the fat boy's head into the wire meshing. He let the racquet fall on the tarmac. He walked towards her, looking straight into her eyes so that if his courage gave out he would be forced to say something. Come over to the burrows, he would say. He would tell her about that place, but the way she raised her head, he suspected she knew it.

She raised her head and opened her mouth, her

72

answer already there. She inhabited that place, was already there, her open mouth like it was for the life-guard when he pressed his hand to her stomach, pushed the salt water out, then put his lips to her lips and blew.

SKIN

The odd fantasies we people our days with; she had just pierced her finger with the knife, and from between the petals of split skin blood was oozing. It was coming in one large drop, growing as it came. Till her detatched face reflects in the crimson.

But in fact the knife had missed her forefinger. It had cut round the gritty root of the lopped-off stem and was now splicing the orb into tiny segments. Her eyes were running. Cracked pieces of onion spitting moisture at her, bringing tears, misting her view of the enamel sink. The sink that was, despite the distortion of tears, as solidly present as it had been yesterday.

She was absorbed in the onion's deceit; its double-take. She had peeled layer upon layer from it and was anticipating a centre. Something like a fulcrum, of which she could say: here the skin ends; here the onion begins. And instead there was this endless succession of them, each like a smaller clenched fist, fading eventually into insignificance. Embryonic cell-like tissue which gave the appearance of a core. But in fact the same layers in miniature. Ah, she sighed, almost disappointed, looking at the handful of diced onion on the draining-board. She gathered these in her hands and shook them into the bowl. She washed her hands, to dispel the damp oily feeling, the acid smell. Then she turned her back on the sink, gazed absently on the kitchen table.

She had an apron on her, something like a smock. Flowers bloomed on it, toy elephants cavorted on their hind legs. There was lace round the neck and a bow-tied string at the back and a slit-pocket across the front into which she could place her hands or dry her fingers. Above it her face, which was uneventfully trim, and just a little plain. She was wearing high-heeled house slippers and an over-tight bra. Her shoulder was shifting uncomfortably because of it. When one rests one notices such things. She was resting. From the diced onions, carrots, chunks of meat, whole potatoes on the draining-board. From the black-and-white pepper tins on the shelf above it.

There were two large windows on the sink side of the room. On the wall opposite was a row of small single-paned windows, high up, near the roof. The midday sun came streaming in the large window from behind her. She saw it as a confluence of rays emanating from her. When she shifted, even her shoulder, there would be a rapid rippling of light and shadow on

the table cloth. Blue light it was, reflecting the blueness of the kitchen decor. For everything was blue
here, the pantry door, the dresser, the walls were
painted in rich emulsion, varying from duck-egg to
cobalt. And the day was a mild early September, with
a sky that retained some of August's scorched ver-
million. The image of the Virgin crossed her silent
vacant eyes. She had raised her hand to her hair and
saw the light break through her fingers. She thought
of the statue in the hall; plastic hands with five plastic
sunrays affixed to each; streaming towards the feet,
the snake, the waterbowl. Mother of Christ.

She had been humming the first phrases of a tune.
She stopped it when she returned abruptly to the
sink, to the window, to the strip of lard— sparrow
meat— hanging outside. She chopped the meat into
neat quarters and dumped them with the vegetables
into a saucepan. She placed the saucepan on a slow-
burning ring. Then she began washing her hands again.
The scent of onion still clung to them. Pale hands,
made plump by activity, swelling a little round the
wrist and round the spot where the tarnished engage-
ment-ring pulled the flesh inwards. She massaged
seperately the fingers of each hand, rapidly and a
little too harshly; as if she were vexed with them,
trying to coax something from them. Their lost freshness.

Several inches of water in the sink; a reflection
there— two hands caressing, a peering face swimming
in the mud-coloured liquid, strewn over with peel.
She grabbed hold of the knife and plunged it, wiping
it clean with her bare thumb and forefinger. And

again came the image— blood oozing, in large crimson drops. But her finger didn't gape. The knife emerged clean.

She pulled the sink plug then, hearing the suck, scouring the residue of grit and onion-skin with her fingers. She dried her hands, walked with the towel into the living-room.

There there was a low-backed modern sofa, two older tattered armchairs and a radiogram piled with magazines. She sat in the sofa, easing herself into its cushioned supports. She fiddled with the radio dial, turned it on, heard one blare of sound and switched it off again. The silence struck her; the chirp of a sparrow outside, clinging to the strip of lard. In another minute she was restless again, leafing through the magazines, flicking impatiently over their pages.

A housewife approaching middle-age. The expected listlessness about the features. The vacuity that suburban dwelling imposes, the same vacuity that most likely inhabited the house next door. But she was an Irish housewife, and as with the whole of Irish suburbia, she held the memory of a half-peasant background fresh and intact. Noticeable in her dealings with the local butcher. She would bargain, oblivious of the demands of propriety. She would talk about childhood with an almost religious awe, remembering the impassioned innocence of her own. And, although house-proud, rigorous tidiness made her impatient; she had a weakness for loose-ends.

And in her the need for the inner secret life still bloomed. It would come to the fore in odd moments. A fragment of a song, hummed for a bar or two, then broken off. A daydream. She would slide into it like a suicide easing himself into an unruffled canal. She would be borne off, swaying, for a few timeless moments. She would hardly notice the return. And for occasional stark flashes, she would be seized by a frightening admixture of religious passion and guilt, bordering on a kind of painful ecstasy; the need, the capacity for religiously intense experience of living; and in consequence of the lack of this, a deep residue of guilt. At times like this she would become conscious of anything red and bloodlike, anything blue or bright, any play of light upon shade.

But if she were asked how she lived, she would have replied: happily. And if she were asked what happiness meant she wouldn't even have attempted an answer.

She found herself rummaging among the magazines searching out one she had been reading yesterday. She recalled a story in it about the habits of Swedish housewives. Certain of them who would drive from their homes between the hours of two and four in the afternoon, out to the country, and there offer themselves to men. The event would take place in a field, under a tree, in a car. And afterwards, they would straighten their clothes, return home to find the timing-clock on the oven at nought, the evening meal prepared. It had disgusted her thoroughly at first glance. But something in it had made her read to the finish. The image, perhaps, of a hidden garden, sculpted secretly out of the afternoon hours, where flowers grew with unimaginable freedom.

Now she was feeling the same compulsion. 'Weekend' was the name, she remembered, selecting one from the pile. She opened it at the centre page. A glaring headline there, in vulgar black print: 'SWEDISH HOUSEWIVE'S AFTERNOON OF SIN'. And a picture; a woman standing by a clump of trees, in a shaded country lane. A man in the distance watching her. A parked car.

She closed it instantly. It had disgusted her again. But as she sat there, the sound of distant cars coming to her from the road, her fingers began drumming impatiently on the wooden top of the radio. Something about it drew her. The sun, the glossy green of the foliage. The man's dark predatory back. Not the cheapness, the titillating obscenity. Not that.

Then she was moving towards the front door. Her tweed walking coat was hanging in the alcove. Outside, rows of starlings laced the telegraph-wires. Motionless black spearheads, occasionally breaking into restless wheeling flights, to return again to their rigid formations. The same expectant stasis in her, her drumming fingers, like fluttering wings. She was a starling. The sudden, unconscious burst of disquiet. The animal memory of a home more vibrant, more total than this. The origin-track; the ache for aliveness.

All the way through the hall, out the front door, her fingers drummed. As she turned the ignition-key in the dashboard the engine's purr seemed to echo this drumming.

Howth was facing her as she drove, answering her desperate need for open spaces. Slim spearlike poplars passed her on her left. Oaks gnarled and knotted to bursting-point. Ash and elder, their autumn leaves discoloured by traffic-dust. She drove mechanically.

She hardly noticed the line of cars coming towards her. Only the earth to her right, a dull metal plate today. Beyond it, as if thrusting through its horizon with a giant hand, the Hill of Howth.

Her forefinger still tapping on the steering-wheel. Scrubbing vegetables had banished most of the varnish from the nail. Today she didn't notice. A car swerved into her lane and away. She had a moment's vision of herself as a bloodied doll, hanging through a sharded windscreen. She drew a full breath and held it, her lungs like a balloon pressing at her breasts.

She pulled in at a causeway that led across marshlands to the open sea. She quenched the engine and gave herself time to absorb the shock of silence. Then she opened the door, got out, her fingers drumming on the metal roof.

Sounds that could have been the unbending of grass or the scurrying of insects. The lapping hiss of tide from the marshlands, its necklace of canals. But now she was here she wasn't sure why she had come. What to do with 'this'— as if the scene before her were some kind of commodity. It was the silence. The sheer pervasiveness of it.

She ran from the car door to the edge of the causeway in an attempt at the abandonment she imagined one should feel. There was a drop there, then mudflats awaiting tide. Nothing came of it however. Only the sense of her being a standing, awkward thing among grasses that crept, tides that flowed. It didn't occur to her to fall, flatten herself with them, roughen her cheek with the ragwort and sea-grass. She began to walk.

There were ships, tankers most likely, on the rim of the sea. As she walked through the burrows she saw hares bounding. She saw the sun, weak, but still potent. She saw a single lark spiralling towards it. She saw, when she reached it, a restful strand dissolve on either side into an autumn haze. It was empty of people.

The sand rose in flurries with her steps. She had worn the wrong shoes— those high-heeled slippers. Useless, she thought, slipping them off.

The sea amazed her when she reached it. Surging, like boiling green marble. Very high too, from yesterday's spring tide. There was a swell, beginning several yards out, that reached her in ripples. Each wave seemed to rise like a solid thing, laced with white foam, subsiding into paltriness just when she felt it would engulf her. Swelling, foaming, then retreating. The sun glistening coldly off it. She felt spray on her cheek. Wet, ice-cold, the feel of church floors, green altar-rails.

She decided to risk a paddle. She glanced round her and saw nothing but a black dot, like a rummaging dog, in the distance. So she opened her coat, hitched up her skirt, unpeeled her stockings. She'd stay near the edge.

She threw them, with her slippers, to a spot she judged safe from the incoming tide. She walked in, delighted with the tiny surging ripples round her ankles. Her feet were soon blue with the cold. She remembered her circulation and vowed not to stay long. But the freshness of it! The clean salt wetness, up around her calves now! It deserved more than just an ankle-paddle. And soon she was in it up to her knees, with the rim of her skirt all sodden. The green living currents running about her legs, the rivers of puffy white foam surrounding her like a bridal wreath. She hitched up her dress then, the way young girls do, tucking it under their knickers to look like renaissance princes, and felt the cold mad abandon of wind and spray on her legs. A wave bigger than the others surged up wetting her belly and thighs, taking her breath away. The feel of it, fresh and painful, icy and burning! But it was too much, she decided. At her age, skirt tucked up in an empty sea.

She turned to the strand and saw a man there, a wet-tailed cocker-spaniel at his heels, bounding in a flurry of drops. She froze. He had seen her, she was sure of that, though his eyes were now on the dog beside him. The sight of his tan overcoat and his dark oiled hair brought a desolate panic to her. The shame, she thought, glancing wildly about for her stockings and shoes.

But the sea must have touched her core with its irrational ceaseless surging. For what she did then was to turn back, back to the sea, picking high delicate steps through its depths, thinking: He sees me. He sees my legs, my tucked-up skirt, the outlines of my waist clearly through the salt-wet fabric. He is more excited than I am, being a man. And there was this pounding, pounding through her body, saying: this is it. This is what the sea means, what it all must mean. And she stood still, the sea tickling her groin, her eyes fixed on the distant tanker, so far-off that its smoke-stack seemed a brush stroke on the sky, its shape that of a flat cardboard cut-out. Around it the sea's million dulled glimmering mirrors.

But she was wrong. And when she eventually turned she saw how wrong, for the man was now a retreating outline, like the boat, the dog beside him a flurrying black ball. And she thought, Ah, I was wrong about that too. And she walked towards the shore, heavy with the knowledge of days unpeeling in layers, her skirt and pants sagging with their burden of water.

HER SOUL

'I've lost my wife' the man said.

'And I've lost my soul'........................

She leaned back on the banisters. The man swayed as he came down, spilling his orange-coloured drink on her dress. But the dress was patterned in broad horizontal stripes like a spinning-top and all of the stripes were some shade of orange so she didn't remark on it. She held on to the banisters swaying, wondering how it had gone so easily.

It hadn't gone the way it should have, like a silver bird flying upwards leaving the shell of her behind, of an aeroplane glinting. It had slipped out of her as if she was a glass and it was the liquid, she filled too full, it slopping down her wet side. And being insubstantial it had disappeared, melted like quick ice, not giving her a chance to grab or shout come back.

Well, she thought.

The music came from the room downstairs and the ecstatic party sounds. She flattened the damp side of her heliotrope dress with her hand.

'My soul' she muttered to the grey suit and the loose neck-tie that was ascending the stairs.

'My undying love', he said and she wondered whether this was taunt or invitation. She was past recognition of witticisms. She looked down the stairs seeing the broad swipes of shadow and the broad swipes of light and thought how easily it could have slipped through one of them. Sidled through, sly thing that it was. Her eyes ran with the shadowed stairs, bumped with them down to the stairs-end closet. Coats hung there, etched and still. Broad folds and shadows. That's it, it slipped, she thought, like a shadow slips when the sun goes in. And every shadow and every fold of cloth became an invitation to her, a door behind which the shadow-world lay, through which one could slip and float and be insubstantial and pure, like gas released from a test-tube, not heavy and swaying like in this bright-light world. That's it, she thought.

Suddenly the shadows tottered and wheeled and the cream-white walls swung dark and bright and she thought she would be blessed with entry into that shadow-world where her soul perhaps was. But then she saw the man with the open tie above her on the stairs tapping the light-bulb.

'My soul', she said thinking it was a party and one must say something.

'My beard and whiskers', he said, tapping the bulb.

'Stop it, will you'. She covered her eyes.

'I'm sorry', he said. 'Have some'.

He held out his hand, proffering a glass. She saw a silver bracelet over the hair on the wrist, then a white cuff and a grey sleeve. At the top of the sleeve was a loose tie and a fattish white neck and brown eyes and a smiling mouth. The eyes were fixed on her left ear and the mouth smiling at something adjacent to it, over her shoulder.

And she fancied, taking the glass, that that was it. Her soul hadn't dripped or flown but had retreated to some point beyond her shoulder; that point towards which people looked, the point posited by his eyes, his eyes that had ripped it from her breast or wherever, from under the heliotrope dress where it should have lain pulsing and whole; had done so because there it was safe, there it was distant.

All the anger at the loss of her soul ran through her so strongly that she imagined she could somehow get it back, that by smashing the glass with her hand on it against the banisters it would somehow appear, reappear with the real pain and the ripped palm and the red sharded pieces of glass.

But she sipped from the glass instead, thinking she would never know, perhaps it's better gone, rolling the whiskey about her palate and her tongue, wondering what to say.

OUTPATIENT

When she came back she was thinner than ever. She had always been thin, but now her thinness seemed to have lost its allure, her mouth seemed extraordinarily wide, all her facial bones prominent. And when he looked at her he stopped thinking of love and began to think of necessary companionship, mature relationship and things like that. It will be better, he told her, when we get the house. And he put his arms around her on the steps and knew that he had married her for that peculiar quality of thinness that had been fashionable that year. Somewhere inside him he felt obscurely angry at her for having let her stock of beauty fade; for standing before him in the same tweed cloak in which she had left, like a thin pear topped by flat brown hair and brown eyes, an oval of skin the colour of thawed snow. He felt cheated.

He also felt virtuous, accepting as he was her flawed self, and only a little ashamed. And all the while she felt his arms around her on the steps she had left and imagined the house to be rectangular, as all houses are, with rectangular rooms and a pebble-dash front. And a garden. There would have to be a garden.

They walked up the steps and up the stairs, past the many flats into their own. She heard the old woman moving round above them. She hasn't died yet, she asked him. No, he whispered, and looked shocked. He told her there was nothing to be ashamed of, that it wasn't as if she had had a breakdown, just that she needed a rest. He asked her what it was like, said that her letters hadn't told him much. She told him that she had seen the Burren and described the burnt mountain landscapes. She told him about St Brigit's Well and described the long line of pilgrims stretching up the mountain and the faded holy pictures inside the grotto and the four crutches of the cripples who had been miraculously cured. Do you believe it, she asked him. Do you believe they were cured? Perhaps, he said, they were never really crippled, or the cure was psychosomatic. But miraculously, she asked, not miraculously? and the word sounded like a peal of trumpets in her ears, she saw the biblical walls tumbling. And he didn't answer, he looked at her quickly once, and then took her by both shoulders and stood back from her, as if complimenting her on something. It did you good, he said, and it will be better this time. Won't it?

She heard the old woman moving again and pictured her wrinkled thin head bending over the one-bar electric fire. He had let his hands drop. They were standing facing one another, neither looking. Mentally she took several steps backwards. She saw two people in a room with three white walls and one orange wall, with blue-coloured armchairs, prints of old Dublin and poster reproductions. There was a hum of traffic through the window from way below. If she had seen it as an extract from a film she would have known it to be the last-but-one scene of some domestic tragedy. And she knew it wasn't going to work once more, she could see the end from the extract, but it wouldn't fail tragically, it would piffle out, with barely a whisper. For she knew that once she could look at herself as if she were another person it would not work, there would be no real pain even. And she discovered to her surprise that she thirsted for pain and reality. What was it about this house, she asked. It's a bargain, he began . . .

He watched her undress as if wondering would her thinness be the same underneath. It was, except that her belly now seemed to sag outwards. She was wearing the tight girlish underwear that always had excited him. He looked at her face as little as possible so as to remain aroused, concentrating on her thin buttocks and stark ribs. He had determined not to sleep, he had determined this should stay even if the rest failed. He decided that her sagging belly was due to her stance. He looked in her face and saw her eyes, unbearably brown and her flat hair. Come, he said.

She was amazed he wanted it. She was gratified in an automatic romantic manner till she gauged his methodic sensuality and knew he was already thinking of children. She determined to disappoint him and lay

91

flat and rigid. She knew he was disappointed but felt the dome of a great heavy bell around her, she looking out through it, at him lying flat and white, staring at the ceiling. Help me, he said. Promise me you'll help me. I can't she said, if you don't help me. What does that mean, he asked. It means there's a space between you and me that no-one can help. No-one, he said. She didn't answer. She was composing an equation, of the sum of her need and the sum of his, of the compound of their ability to give and of the small persistent almighty minus in between. Then she pulled herself from between the covers and went out to wash. We'll go to see the house tomorrow, she heard him say and she noticed how the wretchedness of his voice a moment ago had gone. It sounded common-sense and confident, coming to her in the dark of the bathroom.

He mumbled something and turned on his side, with his back to her, when she returned to the bed. He was well into sleep. But she lay awake staring at the wastes of the ceiling, thinking, I've just come back from a place where people walk three miles to see the miraculous crutches and the rotting mass-cards and he—. Her thought stopped here, blocked by something deadening, momentous, stolid. And he what, she thought. She couldn't praise or blame or hate. She thought instead of the equation again, of the sum of his giving and the sum of hers, of their mutual spaces and the ridiculous pathetic minus round which the worlds hinged. She thought herself, rocked herself to sleep, praying for more, for the miraculous plus. She dreamed of meat. She dreamt she was love-making, rigid against his rapid orgasm and above them was hanging a butcher's half-carcass, swinging between ceiling and floor. Gigot or loin, she wondered. Each rib was curved like a delicate half-bow, white, made stark by the red meat between. She wanted to shake him, and cry out: Look at that dead meat. But it swung above her, silencing her, glowing, incandescent.

The next day he drove her to the house, positively angry now at her silences, more and more repulsed by her battered thinness. It was in a North-side suburb near Portmarnock beach. Streets rose up a hill, breezes came from the unseen sea, the salt air was belied by the system-built houses. They drove up to it and parked on the opposite side. Its facade, she saw, was a large rectangle, half red-brick, half pebble dash. What do you think, he asked. She nodded her head. You'll get nothing better under eight thou, he said. She didn't answer. She suddenly hated him for that abbreviated word. She looked at the house, itself like an abbreviated word, its shape, its texture. Why is it square, she said, why not round? I want to live in a round house, with a roof like a cone, with a roof like a witch's hat. She laughed and heard her laugh echoing strangely in the car. She saw his hands clasping and unclasping, each finger in its curve on the plastic wheel. She stopped the laugh quickly then. But the silence rang with the stopped laugh.

They walked through it and she saw her imagination verified. They walked through the hall, with its regular stairs rising upwards, into the kitchen, which gleamed bright steel. They walked out of the kitchen and up the stairs, through each bedroom and then returned to the kitchen again. What do you think, he asked. She

93

had her back turned to him and she felt the great bell descend on her, its brass tongue falling with a threat she only dreamed of. She turned to his voice, which was tiny and distant, and saw his horror of silence in his set face. She saw her face reflected in his pupil, with enlarged thin cheekbones and a too-wide mouth. Then she longed for the tongue to clang with its trumpetlike peal as she heard him say: We'll look at the garden.

And she saw him open the kitchen door, totally without her fear. She saw through the door the green mound of Howth Head, a long stretch of sea and a thin elongated smokestack of grey cloud. She saw his square back moving towards the backdrop of waste sea and cloud. He was moving to the paltry green rim of hedge at the end, avoiding the mounds of cement-coloured earth, scraping with the toe of his shoe at the resilient ground. When he reached it he turned. And she walked towards him down the calloused garden wanting to tell him that this house had nothing to do with miracles and trumpets, knowing she would not. There was a wind blowing from the sea, ruffling the hedge, his hair and her kilted skirt.

TREE

There were two things he could not do, one was
drive a car, the other was step out of a car. So she was
driving when she saw the tree, she had been driving
all week. He was telling her another point of interest
about the crumbling landscape round them, the landscape with more points of historical interest per square
mile than— something about a woman who was to have
a baby at midnight, but who sat on a rock and kept the
baby back till dawn, an auspicious hour, and the rock
ever after had a dent in it and was called Brigid's—

She saw the tree from about a mile off, since the
road they were driving was very straight, rising slowly
all the time, with low slate walls that allowed a perfect,
rising view. It was late summer and the tree looked
like a whitethorn tree and she forgot about local his-
tory and remembered suddenly and clearly holidays

95

she had taken as a child, the old Ford Coupe driving down the country lanes and the flowering whitethorn dotting the hedges. It would appear in regular bursts, between yards of dull green. It would be a rich, surprised cream colour, it would remind her of a fist opened suddenly, the fingers splayed heavenwards. It would delight her unutterably and her head would jerk forwards and backwards as each whitethorn passed.

Then something struck her and she stopped the car suddenly. She jerked forward and she heard his head striking the windscreen.

'What's—' he began, then he felt his head. She had interrupted him.

'I'm sorry', she said, 'but look at that tree'.

'There are no trees'. His fingers had searched his forehead and found a bump. He would be annoyed. 'This is a limestone landscape'.

She pointed with her finger. His eyes followed her finger and the edges of his eyelids creased as he stared.

'Well there is a tree, then'.

'It's a whitethorn tree', she said. 'It's flowering'.

'That's impossible', he said. She agreed.

The thought that it was impossible made her warm, with a childish warm delight. She felt the hairs rising on her legs. She felt the muscles in her legs glow, stiff from the accelerator. The impossible possible she thought. She knew the phrase meant nothing. She remembered an opera where a walking-stick grew flowers. She thought of death, which makes anything possible. She looked at his long teutonic face, such perfection of feature that it seemed a little deformed.

'But it's white, isn't it'.

'Then', he said, 'it couldn't be a whitethorn'.

'But it's white'.

'It's the end of August'.

She turned the key in the ignition and drove again. She thought of his slight, perfect body beside her in bed, of its recurrent attraction for her. She thought of his hatred of loud sounds, his habit of standing in the background, the shadows, yet seeming to come forward. She thought of how his weaknesses became his strengths, with a cunning that was perhaps native to his weakness. She thought of all the times they had talked it out, every conceivable mutation in their relationship, able and disable, every possible emotional variant, despision to fear, since it's only by talking of such things that they are rendered harmless. She drove the car slowly, on the slight upward hill, the several yards to the pub they had arranged to stop at.

'It is possible'.

'What is'.

'Everything's possible'.

He asked would they go in then.

She opened her door and walked around the car and opened his door. She waited till he had lifted his good leg clear of the car, then held his arm while he balanced himself and lifted out the stiff leg.

She watched him walk across the road and marvelled again at how the stiffness gave him, if anything, a kind of brittle elegance. She saw him reach the pub door, go inside without looking back. Then she looked up the road, curving upwards and the tree off from the road, in the distance. It was still white. Unutterably white.

The pub was black after the light outside. He was sitting by the long bar, drinking a glass of beer. Beside him was another glass, and a bottle of tonic-water. Behind the bar was a woman with a dark western face, ruined by a pair of steel glasses. She was talking, obviously in answer to a question of his.

'Cornelius O'Brien lived in the lower one', she said. 'Owned more than them all put together. A great packer'.

'Packer?'

'Jury-packer' she said, as if it was a term of office.

He leant forward, his face eager with another question. She slipped into the seat beside him. She poured the tonic-water into the glass, wondering why it was he always bought her that. She must have expressed a preference for it once, but she couldn't remember when. Once she drank whiskey, she remembered, and now she drank tonic. And sometime in between she had changed.

'Why did you get me this', she interrupted.

He looked up surprised. Then smiled, a fluid smile. 'Because you always drink it'.

'Once I drank whiskey'

The wrinkles formed in clusters round his eyes.

'I remember. Yes, Why did you stop?'

She drank it quietly, trying to remember, listening to his further question about the crumbling castles. The woman answered, speaking the way children do, using words they don't understand. She used phrases to describe the dead inhabitants of those castles that were like litanies, that had filtered through years to her, that must have once had meaning. She was cleaning a glass and her eyes looked vacant as her mouth spoke the forgotten phrases.

She stared at the ice in her tonic water. She watched it melt, slowly. She wondered about phrases, how they either retain the ghost of a meaning they once had, or grope towards a meaning they might have. Then she suddenly, vitally, remembered the taste of whiskey. Gold, and volatile, filling not the tongue but the whole mouth.

'Whitethorn', she said, loud, out of the blue, as if it were a statement.

The woman stopped cleaning the glass and looked at her. He put his hand round his glass and looked at her.

'Have you come far, then', the woman asked.

He mentioned a town a hundred miles east.

'A long way alright', the woman said. Then she glanced from him to her.

'Is it herself who drives?'

She saw his hand tighten round the glass. She remembered the taste of whiskey. She said:

'He has a bad leg. There are two things he can't do. Get out of a car, and drive a car. But otherwise everything's fine. Isn't that right John?'

He had already gone towards the door. She fumbled in her pocket to find fifty pence. She couldn't and so she left a pound.

He was standing by the door of the car.

'Why did you have to jabber on like that?'

'Why did you order me a tonic?'

'You're impossible'.

'Nothing's impossible'.

'Get in'.

She drove. He swore at her in considered, obscene phrases as she drove. She knew he would swear like that, slowly and sadistically, scraping every crevice of her womanhood, till his anger had died down. So she drove with her eyes on the blaze far up the road, like a surprised fist with its fingers towards the sky, the brilliant cream-white of a dice-cube. As she drove nearer it seemed to swim in front of her eyes, to expand, to explode, and yet still retain its compact white. She could hear their breathing as she drove, hers fast like an animal that is running, his slow, like an animal that must stand in the one place. Then the white seemed to fill her vision and she stopped. She looked at the trunk below the white and the long field between it and the road. Then she looked at him.

He was crying, and his face looked more beautiful than ever through the tears.

'I love you', he said.

'I'm leaving', she said.

'Again?' he asked.

He grabbed her, half angry, half afraid, but she had the door open already and she slipped away. She walked round the car and looked at him.

'I don't—' she began, but her words were drowned by the sudden blast of the horn. His hand was on it, his knuckles white, his body was bent forward as if all his strength was needed to keep the horn pressed. She could hear the awful blare in her ears and could see his lips moving, saying something. She shouted at him to take his hand off and his lips moved again, saying the same something, the same three words. She made out the three words then and turned from his face and ran.

She ran to the slate wall and clambered over it, scraping her shins. She felt the grass under her feet and put her hands over her ears. She was shocked by the sudden silence, like a sudden immersion in water. She was walking, but it was as if through a mental landscape, no sound but the strange humming of her eardrums. She felt she had closed her eyes and found this field, not driven to it. She knew her feet were walking her towards the tree, but it was as if the tree was coming towards her. The landscape rising with each step and each step bringing the landscape nearer. The tree on the hill, with its white made manageable now, small, tangible, familiar. She counted her steps like a little girl does and each step misplaced her hands and rang in her ears. Then something struck her about the tree, not really white, more an off-grey colour. She took three more steps and it came nearer, with the hill behind it, and its blossoms seemed to flap. But blossoms don't flap, she thought, they are still and pristine, they burst or moult, not flap and she must have run then for it came nearer in several large leaps.

And it was there then, bare rough whitethorn with scores of tiny rags tied to each branch, pieces of handkerchief, shirttails, underwear, shift, masquerading as blossom. She thought of people wishing, tying these proxy blossoms. She thought of her and her hope that it had blossomed and them, making it blossom with their hope. She wondered again what hope meant, what impossible meant, but there was less scope to her wondering. She saw faded holy pictures nailed to the bottom of the trunk but couldn't read the pleas written on them. She took her hands from her ears to tear one off and the wail of the horn flooded her again, distant, plaintive, pleading. She tore a picture off, parts of it crumbled in her fingers, but she read 'To Brigid for favours granted, August 1949'. And the horn wailed like pain.

A LOVE

There were no cars in Dublin when I met you again, the streets had been cleared for the funeral of the President who had died. I remembered you talking about him and I thought of how we would have two different memories of him. He was your father's generation, the best and the worst you said. I remembered your father's civil war pistol, black and very real, a cowboy gun. It was that that first attracted me, me a boy beyond the fascination of pistols but capable of being seduced by a real gun owned by a lady with real bullets— I shattered two panes in your glasshouse and the bullet stuck in the fence beyond the glasshouse shaking it so it seemed to be about to fall into the sea and float with the tide to Bray Head. Then you took the gun from me saying no-one should play with guns, men or boys and put the hand that held it in your blouse, under your breast. And I looked at you, an Irish woman whose blouse folded over and was black and elegant in the middle of the day, whose blouse hid a gun besides everything else. But except that you smiled at me with a smile that meant more than all those I would just have been a kid bringing a message from his father to a loose woman. As it was you walked over the broken glass away from me and I stepped after you over the broken pieces to where the view of the sea was and you began to teach me love.

And when we met again there were no cars and the headlines talked about love and guns and the man who had died and I wondered how different your memory of him would be from mine. It was a stupid pursuit since I had no memory of him other than from photographs and then only a big nose and bulging eyes and spectacles but I knew you would be changed and I knew I was changed and I wanted to stop thinking about it.

There were no cars but there were flowers in the giant pots on O'Connell Bridge, there was a band somewhere playing slow music and there were crowds everywhere on the pavement, women mostly who remembered him as something important, women who clutched handbags to their stomachs and stared at the road where the funeral would soon pass. I could sense the air of waiting from them, they had all their lives waited, for a funeral, a husband, a child coming home, women your age, with your figure, they had loved abstractly whereas you had loved concretely with a child like me. That was the difference I told myself but it was probably only that I knew you and I didn't know them. But that had always been the difference, all women had been a mother to someone but you had been a lover to me. And I focused my eyes on the empty street with them and wondered had that difference faded.

I went into the cafe then and it smelt of Dublin, Ireland, the musty femininity of the women waiting on the curb for the men to pass, dead, heroic, old and virginal. I sat by the plate glass window and looked at the shiny chrome expresso machine, a cloud of steam rising from it. A girl in a blue smock with an exhausted face brought me coffee and I felt for the first time that I was back somewhere. I tasted the coffee and got the cheap caffeine bite, details like that, the girl's legs, too thin so the nylons hung in folds around them. Outside I could hear the brass band coming nearer, louder like the slowed step soldiers use in funerals. I knew I was out of step, it was all militarism now, like air in a blister, under the skin, it was swelling, the militarism I had just learned of before, in the school textbooks. Then I remembered something else about him, the man who had died, he had been the centre of the school textbooks, his angular face and his thirties collar and his fist raised in a gesture of defiance towards something out there, beyond the rim of the brown photograph, never defined. And I wondered whether I'd rather be out of step here or in step in London, where the passions are rational. And I felt the nostalgia of the emigrant, but it was as if I was still away, as if here in the middle of it all I was still distant, remembering, apart from it. I shook myself but couldn't get rid of the feeling. Something had happened to me since leaving, something had happened to me long before I left, but then everything changes, I told myself and some things die. So I just looked out the plate-glass window and listened to the slow brass, swelling more all the time.

Then I saw someone looking like you coming down the street towards the cafe and as that someone came nearer I saw it was you, still you, your hair had got a little greyer but still kept that luxuriant brownness, your face had got thinner and fatter, thinner round the cheekbones, fatter round the jaw and neck. You hadn't seen me yet but I couldn't get myself to rise out of the seat so you would see me, I wanted to look at you like you were a photograph. I was remembering that letter of my father's, the only letter, that said you were sick and you did look sick, in the quiet way of bad sicknesses, cancer and the like. And then you opened the glass door and the brass music grew to an orchestra and the door closed and the music faded again and still I couldn't get up. And you were standing over me.

'Neil' you said!
'Yes' I said.
'Well' you said.

106

'Yes' I said again.

And then you sat down beside me, I was a child who isn't saying something, the thin girl came over to take your order. We were the only two in the cafe, you were talking, I was listening to you, quite natural, ordinary things after all. We were different, I was a young adult, you were an old adult, we both fingered coffee cups, mine cold, yours hot. I tried obscurely to remember, I had been an Irish boy with greased hair and a collarless leather jacket, you had been a single woman who kept a guest-house in a town called Greystones and now both of us were neither, my hair was dry and short, it came straight down my forehead and my forehead had a few lines, though people still told me sometimes that I looked sixteen, you were living in a house somewhere on the South Side, you didn't work now though the car keys you squeezed in your palm and the fur sleeves that hung dead from your wrists made you look well-off, in an extravagant, haphazard way.

Then you mentioned the dead man outside.

And somehow it began to come right. I noticed the black silk blouse under the coat, the loose and mottled skin where your neck met your breast. I remembered the nights lying in your old creaking bed that looked out on the sea, our movements like a great secret between us, silent, shocking movements, our silence a guard against my father who had the room down below, our lovemaking a quiet desecration of the holiday town, of the church at the top of the hill, of the couples you fed so properly at mealtimes, of my embarrassed adolescence, the guilt you tried to banish in me, the country, the place, the thing you tried to hit at through me you taught me to hit through you. And all the time for me there was my father lying underneath, cold most likely, and awake and I wanted him to hear the beast I was creating with you, I wanted him to hear it scratching, creaking through to him from above, for your body was like the woman he must have loved to have me, I had seen her in those brown faded photographs with a floppy hat and a cane, in a garden, like you but fatter, with a lot of clothes that came off, the coloured dresses and blouses first, then the white underclothes, dampened under the armpits, between the legs. And when you undressed on the beach and I watched you from the road, watched each thing falling in a bundle on the sand, you could have been her, you could have been anyone's mother only you were naked with a belly that drooped a little and a triangle of hair underneath it. Only that when you saw me you didn't shy from my frightened stare, you smiled. That smile began it. But what perpetuated it was something outside, my mathematical father lying sleepless on his bed, your civil-war gun, rosaries, that rain-soaked politician with his fist raised, clenched. Against something. Something.

The brass band seemed much nearer now, going ahead of the same politician's cortege, ceremonial, thudding slow brass. I was watching you drinking your coffee. The brass music was cascading about you. I looked at the thin part of your face, you had no make-up on, your eyes looked almost ordinary. You were different and the same, I was different and the same, I knew that that is how things happen. And yet I'd met you because I wanted something more. We are all different threads, I told myself and once we had woven each other's threads into something like a bow. Once.

'Well'.

We were stuck on that word. Then I plunged.

'What are we going to do then, before I go back?'

'Back where?'

And I don't know whether you wanted to know, but I told you it all, about the hairdresser's in Kensal Rise, the women who tipped me pound notes if I touched their plump shoulders and told them they were too young for a blue rinse.

'Is that what you do'.

'Yes'.

And I told you about the cockney queen I shared a room with who I despised but who could be warm when—

'And don't you act now—'

And yes, I told you about the sweaty revues, revue being synonymous with theatrical sex, I told you about the empty stages where we rehearsed in our underwear and fingered each other's goosepimples, simulated copulation. Then I stopped, because you were drinking your coffee again and your unmadeup face looked sad, like an adolescent, the one I had been. And for a moment I was the experienced one, I clutched the gun, under my breasts, between the sheaves of my black blouse.

'We'll go to Clare. Lisdoonvarna'.

'Why there', I asked.

'I am past my prime. They are places for people past their prime'.

And I wondered should you say 'prime' or 'primes', I thought of all the hotels and guest-houses I had never been to. I knew middle-aged people went to those places and met men and took the waters and married maybe and drank sherries looking at the Atlantic, in bars that were probably closed now for De Valera's death.

'It's Autumn and everyone there will be past their prime. I want to see the bachelors court the spinsters. I want to take the waters. I want to drive in a Morris Minor past the Burren and look at the unusual flowers'.

There was an accusation in your voice as if you were trying to tell me something, something I didn't want to hear. I thought maybe you wanted to fit yourself, label yourself and I wondered would your conformity be as bizarre as my attempts at it had been.

110

You talked about happiness then, a murderous happiness that followed you round like a pet dog. And I looked at you, you had pressed your unpainted lips together, the blood had gone out of them and I saw the need for happiness that had ravaged you, I wondered what deity it was that would label you old maid or spinster when you had once pressed that happiness on me. Then I heard the band outside, so loud now, and the cortege was passing and the band was playing the old nationalist tunes to a slow tempo. I felt I was watching an animal dying through the plate-glass window, an animal that was huge, murderous, contradictory and I looked up at your face, not much older really than when I had last seen you and I looked out the plate-glass window again at the funeral of the man I didn't remember, the man you would have remembered. I wondered what your memories were, your associations. And I looked at your eyes, bare and washed clean and I somehow knew.

We walked outside then and the brass music became a deafening thud. We walked slowly down the street, we couldn't talk, the music was so loud. I bought a newspaper at the corner of Abbey Street and saw a headline about the funeral that was crawling along beside us. We passed a TV sales shop where a crowd of people were staring at a white screen, staring at the death being celebrated behind them.

As I remember you I define you, I choose bits of you and like a child with a colouring-book, I fill you out. The car-keys are swinging on your finger, your forefinger and thumb choose one, insert it in the lock and your whole hand tenses in the turning. Your car is like you said, a Morris Minor. It's grey and covered in dents and the chrome is rusty. Your hand turning is reddish, sunburnt, which accentuates more its many creases. Then a man-sized watch and the sleeve of your coat where the fur has rubbed off.

Once it was desire I filled you out with, not memory. You were a blown-up photograph to me, a still from a film. I brought the youthful sullenness I learnt from the hit songs to you. I ate chips before I came to you, my fingers stank of vinegar, my breath of nicotine. And you played with me, you let me fill you out, you played Ava Gardner to my James Dean. But I chose, I was arbitrary, I took what I wanted. Your brown hair, your anxious mouth, your bare feet— on the straw bedroom mat. I took some and left the rest, I didn't know what the rest meant, I didn't know what varicose veins meant or fallen arches or lace curtains, respectability, spinsterhood. I plead guilty but ignorant, I didn't know what woman meant.

'Can you drive?'

I said no. I said I would like to, I would like to feel machinistic and free but my father never drove so no-one taught me.

'What do you mean', you asked 'Machinistic—'

And I hadn't known what I meant, I got confused, I said something about the wheel driving, following the white line. Then you were quiet for a while, whether from tactfulness or not I don't know and then—

'I wasn't made for cars'

I didn't believe you, you had shaped this car to fit you. You drove it like it fitted you, through the city that was empty, that had put its best side out for the man who had died. The streets were clean, the buildings were respectful, they seemed to curtsy before us as you drove. Then they got thinner and thinner and we were on the dual carriageway, driving west.

'I idolised him once'.

I meant to ask you about your sickness but the words wouldn't come. So you talked while you drove, abstracted talk.

'I was taught to idolise him, everyone was. I remember standing at meetings, holding my father's hand, waving a tricolour, shouting Up Dev. My father wore a cloth cap and a trenchcoat, everyone did then'.

Your eyes were squinted towards the road as if you saw what you were remembering on it.

'His face was like a schoolteacher's. Or maybe all schoolteachers tried to look like him. You could never see his eyes clearly because of his glasses. They were the first thing you noticed after his nose'.

We were passing Monasterevin. The town looped in

a semi-circle round your car.

'Have you ever been to the West?'

'No', I said.

'You'll never understand this country till you have'.

Your voice sounded older, consciously older, something valedictory in it that made me remember the night my father took you out and me with him as his fifteen years old son, mature enough for adult company, my father being a lecturer in maths and a widower, a natural partner for you who was single, who kept the guesthouse he stayed in. We went to a variety in Bray where a Scottish comedian told Irish jokes and a youth with a guitar sang Lonnie Donegan songs and two girls with a ukelele sang George Formby and kicked their legs on either side of the stand-up mike. And afterwards we went for a meal in the Royal Hotel, we ate roast beef and drank sherry. I poured your sherry with the distance he had trained me in and I sat at the far end of the table while you both talked, he at length, you with many pregnant pauses. You talked about life, about friends in public life, who you knew of through your father, who he knew of through his work, he prided himself on both his aloofness from the world and his reserved contact with it. You were beautiful and intimidating in a navy dress and shawl and while in your silences you spoke to me, me in my greased hair and the suit I was told to wear, in your conversation you spoke to him and you managed the pretending so adroitly that in the end I was fooled and I screamed at you afterwards and it took three days for our mutual secret to build up again between us, for me to hold the you I wanted in my unwashed arms, selfishly and viciously, for you to tell me again about love and irreligion, about other countries where women are young at the age of thirty-nine and boys are men at fifteen.

'Are you happy?'

'Sometimes', I said.

'You used to be. You used to be very quiet, very joyful and very sullen'.

We were passing Portlaoise, the barbed-wire towers of the prison and the red wall of the mental hospital.

'It was all in your face', you said. 'In the way your snub-nose twitched—'

And we both laughed then, it sounded stupid but we laughed and your laugh was like a peal, you could have been standing in the broken pieces of glass again, beside the glasshouse, laughing. I tightened my nose like a rabbit the way I used to do, then I flushed in embarrassment doing it and that made you laugh louder, so loud that you began coughing and had to stop the car and wipe your mouth. There was blood on the kleenex you wiped it with.

'We're different', you said.

'Yes', I said. And you looked at me and giggled again. Like someone very young. Too young. You put your arms around me and kissed my face and I stayed very quiet, feeling you again, smelling you again. Your lips opened on my cheek and I could hear a tiny whistle off your breath.

'Aren't we?'

'Yes', I said, 'We're different' and I kissed you back so you could feel how different. But you stopped me.

'Don't try and change me'.

'How could I?'

'You could', you said, 'You could change me back'.

But you were happy then, weren't you? You began to drive faster, swerving gaily to avoid pigeons. You asked me about myself and my father and I answered both as well as I could. You still coughed every now and then and once you had to stop the car, your whole body tensed as if you were in pain. Your fingers clenched the wheel, they seemed to get even thinner and the bones on the backs of your hands were thin, leading like a scallop to the fingers. But you got over it then, you began to drive, you told me not to mind you, that you were only dying, its a common complaint and you laughed like before and I laughed with you. Then we stopped in a pub for a drink and I drank a gin while you drank a pint of stout and the barman remarked on how it's normally the other way round.

When we were driving again we saw a fat girl standing by a petrol-pump following every car that passed her with her eyes and thumb. You wanted to stop but

I didn't let you, I thought she'd come between us and the laughing. So we drove on and I had a clear view of the disappointment in her large blue eyes as she fumbled with her handbag, realising the car wasn't going to stop after all. And I felt sorry for a moment but your mad peculiar gaiety filled the car again and stopped me feeling sorry.

When we came to Limerick you got quieter and I thought we were stopping since it was almost dark. But you said that you hated it there and you drove on till we came to a sign saying Lahinch and a street that was flanked by burrows and summer houses. You stopped. It was fully dark. We were on the street of a seaside town. I could see a beach at the end of the street, then sea, a different sea from the one we had left. But then all seas are the same, I thought and when we walked down to the beach and watched the tide sucking off the long strand I saw it was the same, like the one that had washed your guest-house.

I began to feel it all again, the seaside town, you beside me, wild and intractable and almost old, the bed and breakfast signs, the guesthouses. In the bars men stared at us, men that looked like weekend golfers but I didn't mind, you drank your guinness while I drank my gin, you talked about happiness so much that I had to tell you to stop.

And then we went to a guest-house and it was like yours, it had a grey granite front weeping from the sea-breeze, like yours except that it was a man that signed us in, held out the guest book for us with large, country hands. You paid.

I went behind you up the stairs. Your breathing was so heavy that it sang in my ears. And then we were in the room and it was so bare, there were two beds, a wash-hand basin, a Virgin and a cinema poster, so seductively bare. You asked me to turn while you undressed. My face must have shown my surprise because before I could answer you turned. And I watched you, I saw your clothes form a little heap around your feet, I saw your shoulders that were very thin and your waist that was almost fat now and your buttocks and your legs. And your skin told me you were definitely older. When you were in your nightgown you turned.

'Come on', you said.

There was a knowledge burning through both of us, it was like the yearning that had been there years before, a secret, like blood. But it wasn't a yearning, it

118

was a question and an answer. You knew that with every garment you took off you were stepping into a past self, a self that had that yearning and you could see from my face that I knew too.

'Come on', you said again.

And I took off my clothes and I wore the nakedness I had worn for you, I was a boy then, and I took off your nightdress so you could wear it too.

I didn't look at you, I put my arms around you, standing there, both of us were breathing, our chests touching. You stepped backwards towards the bed.

'Come on', you said.

And we were on the bed, the sea was breathing outside like a woman, we were moving together but I wasn't thinking of you, not you now anyway, I was thinking of you before, of the time he brought you out, the second time, the time after which something finished for me and for you and for him too maybe. He brought you to the Great Northern Hotel this time, and me, there were meal-tables there and a small space for dancing to a small three-piece band. And the meal was like before, you laughing with him and being silent every now and then and me pouring sherry for both of you, in good suit and greased hair. And when the meal was finished the reddish lights came on and the dancing began. The band played waltzes and both of you moved across the floor among other shapeless couples, you beautiful, him tall and supremely confident of something as he waltzed. And I sat there looking and saw him for the first time not as my father who wrote equations on sheets of paper into the night and knew a lot about things like sea-shells but as someone young and agile who had the same yearning for you as I had. And as I drank the sherry that you both had left I began to cry, I felt older than him, insanely older, I had the knowledge of you that made him dance so gracefully, that made that difference in him. Then I drank more sherry and saw his hands around your waist almost touching at the back and I knew people do that when they waltz but I began to hate him as I would hate someone my age. Then again I saw his eyes, distant and kind of hopeful, more hopeful than whenever he had looked at me and as I knew the yearning that was behind them I stopped my hate and felt baffled, sad, older than I could bear. The band was playing the Tennessee Waltz I remembered and I tried to catch your eye but you were looking the other way, looking strict, virginal, leonine. And then I felt the huge resentment, I couldn't do anything with it, my hands were shaking and I knew something was going to end. And you both came back and I pushed the bottle onto the floor with my hand so it would break, so nobody would know how much I had drunk, hoping it would look like an accident. But the crash was loud and everyone stared and he, my father, lost what he had had with you and went white, and shouted at me and you looked quickly at me and I felt I was a child, being chastened publicly. And later I lay in your bed with this huge resentment and hate. You were asleep when I heard him coming up the first floor landing and opening the toilet door. And I got up and you were still asleep, I took the gun from your drawer and went down and stood outside the toilet door. And when I heard the chain pull and I knew he was standing buttoning his fly I raised your civil-war gun and fired quickly four times into the door. And there were four bangs and four rapid thuds and I saw each shot wedging, hardly piercing the mahogany. And I ran upstairs knowing something had finished and I gave you the gun and cursed you quietly because it didn't work—

And then I stopped remembering, you were underneath me, I had come inside you in the room in Clare. Your arms were around my neck, hard, rigid and you said what I was remembering, 'It's finished' you said. And you kissed me tenderly and I kissed you back so you could feel how different we were. And I got from your bed quietly, you were exhausted, turning to sleep already. I lay in my own bed listening to the sea outside me, listening to your breathing. There was a luminous statue of the Virgin over you on the wall and a cinema poster. It said I WAS HAPPY HERE in bold letters and showed a woman in a romantic pose looming over a matchbox version of the town we were in. Then I looked at you and saw the eiderdown rising each time you breathed and your body clenching itself every now and then as if you were dreaming of pain. And I knew it had ended but I still thought to myself, maybe tomorrow—

And tomorrow you got up and drove, you drove to the town you had told me about, where the bachelors and the spinsters come, where you take the waters. We passed the fat girl again on the road but you didn't stop. And the town was like any other holiday town only more so, with its square of hotels and its peeling wooden verandas and old-fashioned cane chairs lining the verandas.

We stopped in the square. It looked strange to me, a holiday town that's inland. I said this to you, why no sea and you said 'There's the sulphur waters'.

We walked up the street a little. A man stared. I bought a guide-book in a shop. I thought of water and holidays, why they go together. Every building seemed to imply a beach, but there was none. It was as if the sea had once been here, but retreated back to Miltown Malbay, leaving a fossil. Somewhere a front door banged.

It was saying something to us, you were saying something, saying This is it, is me, always has been, the

122

part of me you never saw, didn't want to see. And I believed it then, I knew you had always been coupled in my mind with hotels, with cane-chairs and ball-and-claw armchairs. And I crossed the square and bought a paper and read more about the President who had died, but in small print now.

We drove out to the Spa, to a building that looked like a Swiss hotel, but with a river that seemed to come from underneath it. You asked me did I want to come in and I said no, so you went through the two glass doors alone. I sat in the car wondering whether you drank the waters or bathed in them. A couple passed, wearing suits that must have been too hot for the weather. I shouted at them 'Do you drink the water', I shouted, 'or swim in it'. The man looked at me and threw his hands up uncomprehendingly. I watched them going through the glass doors and imagined a room with a clean tiled floor through which flowed brackish, slow water. I imagined you taking your clothes off with a lot of older men and women and I watched from the side as you dipped yourself into the spa waters among people who had the minor complaints of middle-age to wash off, who had made the act of faith in water. But then, I might have been quite wrong, maybe you sat on a wooden bench in a line with other people and drank the brackish water from a tap.

And I knew it was definitely ending anyhow and that I should forget for your sake the peculiar yearning that sprang in me when my cock sprang to attention in my tight trousers that day you put the gun between your breasts into your blouse. You called it love, I remember. And it must have been.